VIVA REAPER!

VIVA REAPER!

B.J. HOLMES

A Black Horse Western

ROBERT HALE · LONDON

ISBN 0 7090 5782 2

Robert Hale Limited
Clerkenwell House
Clerkenwell Green
London EC1R 0HT

Photoset in North Wales by
Derek Doyle & Associates, Mold, Clwyd.
Printed and bound in Great Britain by
WBC Book Manufacturers Limited,
Bridgend, Mid-Glamorgan.

Author's Note

The present book is a work of fiction spun around the following piece of known western history. Yellowed newspaper clippings from a remote date in the last century note that three bandits charged with murder were released for lack of evidence from Juarez Jail, Mexico. Those same file clippings also record that shortly afterwards their bodies were discovered. Someone had stalked and methodically despatched them one by one. It was never learned who had dispensed the justice that the renegades had evaded in court.

Maybe the answer went something like this ...

For three straight-shooters from the old outfit:
Llyn, Clive and Chris

ONE

Some guys don't talk much. Jonathan Grimm was that sort. Born a Scot he didn't see reason for wasting anything, words included. To boot, the occupation he pursued was, by its very nature, a lonely one. The guy on the horse behind him didn't say much either, only his reason was he was dead. Louis Whitey Burdick, one-time bank robber, one-time rapist, one-time murderer, now a full-time corpse.

Grimm grunted with relief when he saw the speck that signalled a town ahead. The concern was not so much for himself but for his horse. Earlier in the day the animal had acted up all of a sudden, trodden awkwardly and then developed a limp. He had dismounted and checked it over. Some years back he had run his own horse ranch so he knew something of their care. But he didn't have to be an expert to know his animal needed to rest the leg and there was no chance of that in the back end of nowhere. From that point on he had stayed out of the saddle and allowed the animal to walk at its own slow pace.

It pained him to see the animal, an Andalusian

grey of normally proud bearing, reduced to a head-hanging hobble. Dearly wanting to get the ailments tended to as soon as possible, he had repeatedly scanned the wobble of heat haze in the hope of some kind of settlement whenever the configuration of land had revealed new terrain ahead. Always in vain, till now.

'Won't be long, pal,' he said when he sighted the settlement and let his horse follow its nose in the direction of water. Both animals and he were thirsty, hungry and covered in dust. He could smell himself and he didn't like that either. Mind, didn't smell as much as the former Mr Burdick. A meagre consolation.

Well, he hadn't kidded himself it was going to be easy. He had chosen the bounty-hunting trail for a passel of reasons, none of which included the notion of 'easy'. Trails were long, dusty and lonely. And there was always the chance of getting your head blowed off. Like the guy behind him had tried to do.

He hadn't wanted to kill the feller but the way the bozo had been behaving, throwing his lead, he kind of insisted that that was the way he wanted it to be, so the man known as the Reaper had obliged. When the chips were down it didn't really matter which way he took them in, just as long as he got paid. And, at the moment, he needed paying. Hadn't seen hard dollars in his fist for the best part of a season. As he'd reminded himself before now, he wasn't in it for 'the easy'.

Reaching the town he stopped at a trough and

allowed the animals to get at the scummy liquid. As the horses satiated themselves he took off his hat, smoothed the long hair that hung over his collar, and looked the town over. A sign explained to the world that it went under the name of Constitution, further proclaiming it to be the county seat. That figured. From where he stood he could tell it was bigger than most settlements he had seen this side of the Pecos: a wide choice of saloons, banks, a court house, railroad depot. Even in parts had a sidewalk of flattened limestone, the sure sign of a place that thought itself important.

He pulled the horses away from the water before they ailed through overgorging, and led them by the reins up the main drag till he came to a livery stable.

'Anybody home?' he queried loudly through the open doorway.

A young man came to the opening and blanched at the sight of the corpse.

'Don't worry about him,' Grimm said. 'He ain't gonna cause no trouble.' He pointed to the foreleg of his own mount. 'I got a lame horse here. I'd like him stalled and a veterinary surgeon to check him out. I got things to do. Can you handle that for me?'

The youngster eventually managed to draw his eyes from the grisly cargo on the second horse, and looked down at the leg on the first animal. 'Sure thing. Horse doctor's a piece along the street.'

Grimm took out a couple of silver dollars and

pushed them into the fellow's shirt pocket. 'Fine. There's something to be going on with. By the by, name's Grimm. That's me, not the horse.'

The lad nodded, not seeing the humour. 'Folks call me Andy,' he said bleakly.

'OK, Andy, let's get him into a stall.'

When the horse was quartered Grimm looked once more at the leg. 'Sure hope it's nothing more than a strained tendon.' After he had unbuckled the cinch and hoisted off the saddle he saw something else and cursed. Removing the saddle had revealed sores along the animal's back.

'That's what you get for letting your tack get dirty,' he said, more in reprimand to himself than to the young man. He'd had a pretty rough week out on the high plains with little chance to attend to either his own or his horse's hygiene. 'I knew he was uneasy over something. It was being agitated in the first place that made him stumble and crook his leg. Well, that needs attention too: cleaning and treating.'

'I'll get Doc Kirby,' Andy said.

Grimm stroked his horse's muzzle. 'While you're doing that I'll get shuck of my cold freight. That's a job needs attending to pronto. Where's your law office?'

The young man accompanied him outside and pointed up the street. 'Couple of blocks on the left. Jed Berringer's marshal. Meantime I'll get the doc.'

Minutes later Grimm was outside a substantial building labelled 'County Law Office'. He tied the reins to the hitchrail, ignoring the sniffy looks of folks who had stopped on the sidewalk to view the horse's odious burden.

Those in his path moved aside as he heavy-footed towards the office. He rapped on the door and accepted the invitation to 'come in' bellowed from behind the ritzy polished glass.

The man behind the desk looked more like a duded-up bank teller than a lawman in appearance, in keeping with the jim-dandy town which constituted his bailiwick.

'Marshal Berringer?'

'That's me, pilgrim. What can I do for you?'

'Name's Grimm. Jonathan Grimm.'

'Ah, a gentleman of the South,' the lawman said. 'Or I'm no judge on a man's manner of talk. The Lone Star, I'll warrant.'

'Not far out,' Grimm said. He'd spent many years in the States, eventually settling in Texas, and had lost some of his Scots burr along the way. 'Bounty chaser,' he continued, irritated by the linguistic diversion and anxious to get to the matter in hand. 'Got a renegade out there. Rode under a variety of sobriquets but you've probably got him filed under Louis Burdick. That's what he's called on this here poster.'

As Grimm fished the crumpled reward paper from his pocket for verification, the lawman looked nervously at the window. 'Will he be OK out there? Is he dangerous?'

'Not any more.'

'You mean he's securely manacled?'

'No, I mean he's securely dead.' Grimm

smoothed out the poster on the desk top and pointed to the relevant information. 'Louis Burdick alias, etc., etc. The usual thing. That's the important bit: two grand.'

'An ugly looking yahoo,' the lawman concluded.

'Smells even worse,' Grimm added, keeping his finger pointing at the dollar digits. 'See? Two grand.'

The man looked back at the window as things sunk in. 'He smells?'

'Yeah. If you don't get him off the street pretty quick I figure this is the kind of burg that will slap a public health charge on you or me or somebody.'

Outside the lawman wrinkled his nose as he surveyed the dead man from a respectful distance. 'I think you'd better lead your horse this way, Mr Grimm. Help me get the deceased over to the mortician and then I'll send out a wire to get clearance on the payment of bounty.'

Grimm nodded. That figured too. This was the kind of place that didn't have undertakers; it had morticians. Following the appropriate lodging of the corpse, he returned to the livery stable with Burdick's horse in tow. Neither the ostler nor the sawbones were yet on the scene so he found a vacant stall for the extra horse.

Then, while he was still in his own trail muck, he set to cleaning his own mount, a task he rarely left to others. He found a pump out back, drew some water and was bathing the broken skin on the saddle area when a voice boomed from the doorway. 'Where's the patient?'

He turned to see a frock-coated man with a bag standing in the doorway.

'Over here, Doc.'

They shook hands, exchanged names and Grimm led him over to his mount.

'An Andalusian,' the doctor observed. 'A magnificent animal.'

'Good stock,' Grimm confirmed, 'and a trusty mount.' He went on to explain the grey's ailments. 'I don't reckon it's a fracture as he's covered a few miles in the condition.'

'We shall see, Mr Grimm.' The doctor put down his bag and, after he had made friends with the horse, examined the saddle sores.

Then he led the animal outside. He had the horse trot towards him on a loose rein, noting the animal's head movements as well as the obvious difficulty it had with its left foreleg.

'Injury only apparent in the one leg,' he observed as he returned the reins to its owner. He bent down and examined the foot, feeling for heat. Then he took out a small hammer from his bag. 'He a trustworthy animal?'

'If I've got him, yes.'

'In that case, hold him steady.'

Grimm spoke to the grey, reassuring him. When he was sure the animal was secured the doctor picked up the hoof and systematically tapped it.

'You're right, Mr Grimm,' he concluded. 'There's no fracture. But the tendon is badly sprained. As you have guessed, it didn't help none walking him on it but I figure that was unavoidable. Obviously I'm gonna have to strap the thing up. The upshot is, he can't be ridden for a spell.'

'I was aiming to stay over a few days anyways,' Grimm explained.

'I'm talking about a couple of weeks, not days,' the doctor countered. 'Not if you want your animal to mend properly.'

Grimm took the news philosophically. He was not surprised at the prognosis and, with a couple of grand coming in, he could afford a long stop over if it was required. 'No problem,' he said. 'You do what's necessary, Doc.'

He leaned against the side of the stall and watched the medic clean and bind the leg. Then the doctor swabbed the saddle sores with disinfectant and applied antiseptic powder.

'OK,' the doctor said when he had finished. 'I'll drop in each day to look him over. The strapping on the leg needs to be changed regularly. Then, once the open wounds on the back have healed I'll harden the area with surgical spirit.'

'How much do I owe you?'

'You got the look of a square joe. Pay me when the treatment's finished.' He looked at his watch. 'Now I'll be on my way. Got another couple of cases to see before nightfall.'

They shook hands and Grimm watched him disappear through the doorway.

'Regular guy,' he observed, then turned to the ostler. 'You got a decent hotel here? If I'm stopping over a spell might as well do it in comfort.'

* * *

Shortly he was writing his name in the register in the lobby of an imposing hotel. The best in town according to the desk clerk, who decorated his boast by pointing out the establishment was currently host to a treaty commission from Washington passing through.

The place was expensive but it was one of the ways Grimm rewarded himself after a long haul: a lingering bath, a full meal and good pipe of tobacco. He was down to his last cents but he was in line for a good pay-day so, what the hell?

TWO

Come sun-up the next morning he checked his horse then took a walk along the main drag, noting as he passed that the law office wasn't open yet. Back in the still-quiet hotel he sat in the lobby and lit up a pipe. There were some newspapers and magazines on the table and, as he waited for the staff to energize and prepare breakfast, he flicked casually through them. Casually, that is, until something caught his eye: an article on the search for conspirators involved in the assassination of Lincoln.

Some years had passed since the awful event, but they were still at it. Following the killing of Booth they had caught and summarily dispensed with many they had claimed to be involved. It was still his feeling that the real culprits were behind the witch-hunt itself. As time passed, the more difficult it was becoming to unearth the real facts. He was sure now the truth would never be known.

His mind went back to that dreadful time. Following the War Between the States, chance had seen to it that he had been serving in the capacity of a presidential messenger.* Effectively the job was that of a bodyguard but he worked under the label of presidential messenger, owing to the fact that Lincoln didn't sanction bodyguards for his person. The great man had said if someone was out to get him they would. Wise in so many things, he had been right about that too.

In the confusion following the assassination Grimm, or Connor as he was then, had been suspected of complicity merely on the strength of his Southern links – he'd spent some years in Texas and had fought his war in a Confederate uniform. After the ceasefire Lincoln had had a policy of incorporating Confederates into the administration as part of what he called his policy of reconciliation.

Snag was virtually all the staff in the White House had been Yankees and the cry of 'Confederate Plot' had been their immediate reaction when the nation's leading figure had died in the dingy room opposite Ford's Theatre. In that atmosphere the young man had quickly realized that his innocence would stand for little against the call for blood by well-placed establishment bastards who were looking for a scapegoat; and so he had lit a shuck. A mistake? Maybe; but he still figured not. Especially when they started shooting at him.

Getting as far from Washington as possible he'd reverted to his mother's maiden name of

* See *Comes the Reaper* (Hale, 1995)

Grimm. From then on circumstances could have pushed him in any direction but as it panned out they'd edged him into hitting the bounty-hunting trail. It brought him his keep and kept him on the move – away from civilization. In his new persona he'd kept his hair uncut and grown a droopy moustache. That was some years ago and so far he hadn't been recognized; and, until his recent unprofitable patch, he'd made enough dinero to get by.

But it was a worry that they were still after Tom Connor. He had been banking that he would have been forgotten now the dust had settled on that sad chapter in US history. But the newspaper in that hotel in Constitution told otherwise. Anyways, the way things were, nobody had recognized him roving the wilderness. And, as there was no good likeness of him on record, there was no reason why anybody should.

He ruminated over the newspaper article until he was called to the dining-room where, in his trail clothes, he looked a shade out of place amongst the soberly-garbed politicians and other expensively dressed patrons.

*   *   *

After breakfast he was back at the law office and this time it was open.

'Anything through on the bounty?' he asked the lawman, who was rubbing his eyes as he tended to the coffee pot hissing on the stove.

'Not yet, Mr Grimm. I wired yesterday, as soon as we'd deposited the deceased at the mortician's. Shouldn't take long. But you know what these pen-pushers are like.' He nodded to a tin mug. 'Join me for a morning coffee? Top quality Java.'

'Obliged.'

'Sit yourself down.'

'Fine town you got here,' Grimm said, after a few hesitant sips of the steaming black liquid.

'Yes. Place really took off when we got designation as the county seat. Court, local government offices. The building of those places brought some much needed employment to the town. Got some state senators living hereabouts too. And the place is still growing. Even have top-drawer dignitaries stopping by. Got some Washington politicians in town at the moment.'

'Yeah. Seen 'em at the hotel where I'm staying.'

'You at the big hotel? Hey, you'll be running up a hefty tab there.'

Grimm chuckled. 'I got two grand coming, ain't I?' He took another sip of his coffee.

They spoke a little longer, with Grimm avoiding divulging too much about his background, then he left for a walk around the town to kill time. Sure was a fine place. Well-gowned ladies, fine-suited gentlemen. Substantial public buildings. If it hadn't have been for the heat and dust coming in from the plains it could have been some Eastern burg.

He bought a drink in an elegant saloon across the street from the law office and sat at the window through which he could watch developments. He always felt edgy until he'd got his money squarely in his fist. Eventually he was rewarded by the sight of a telegraph operator making his way to Berringer's place.

He finished his drink and hastened over to the office only to find the lawman wearing a stern face. 'Bad news, Mr Grimm. Just got a message on the wire. Bounty ain't as much as you was figuring.'

'How much?'

'Five hundred.'

'Five hundred?' Grimm echoed. He pulled out the fading reward poster he had been toting and slapped it on the desk. 'Says two grand here.'

'It's outa date, I'm afraid. Here, see for yourself.' He pushed the wire across for Grimm's inspection. 'Seems Burdick was more mouth than anything else. Everybody thought he was the leader of the bunch but his two cronies have been caught and it's clear from the depositions that he was nothing but a poor third fiddle.'

Grimm thought of the corpse lying in the undertaker's. 'Well the juice-brain has sure paid for his big mouth.'

Then, his thoughts moved to his own situation. 'Hell, I was on that critter's trail for over two months. Now – zilch.' He moved to the window and looked across the street. 'Booked into your snazzy hotel yonder too. And got doctoring fees to pay. Not to mention sundries like quartering my horse.'

'Look on the bright side, Mr Grimm. You got

five hundred dollars coming. 'S more'n I make in a month of Sundays.'

'When do I get that?'

'Take a couple of days to clear through the bank. Shouldn't be any problem.'

Grimm took out his wallet and made a quick check of his meagre funds. 'Can you recommend cheap lodgings? I'm gonna have to check out of your fancy hotel for a start.'

'You'll find several drovers' lodgings on the edge of town. But can't guarantee you won't have fleas for company.'

Grimm thought on it. 'In the meantime I'm claiming Burdick's gear. Leastways, he'd got a good saddle. Guns and horse will pull a few dollars.'

'I suppose they're rightfully yours.'

'You're darn tooting they're rightfully mine. I'm down to my last cents. Need some hard bucks pronto.'

*   *   *

He got his hands on the outlaw's tackle and hauled it round to the classiest saloon. He organized a quick auction with the patrons and managed to pull in a hundred dollars. A good chunk of that would go on his bills, but it was better than nothing.

While eating lunch he thought through his options. So occupied was he that he paid scant attention to the other guests, including the treaty commissioner who occasionally looked quizzically his way from across the room.

Eventually, the politicians rose and made to leave, talking quietly. Near the door one broke from the main group and leant over to Grimm. 'Excuse me, young man, have we met?'

Grimm looked up at him. 'Don't think so, sir.'

The senator shook his head slowly as he scrutinized the seated man's features. 'I've been looking at you from time to time from over yonder. There surely does seem something mighty familiar about your face.' He backed away a step and masked Grimm's moustache with his hand for a moment before continuing. 'But I don't recall the facial hair. Delaware, maybe? You been to Delaware?'

'No, sir.'

'Then it must be Washington.'

Grimm forced a laugh. 'The next time I go that far East will be the first, sir.'

The senator chuckled. 'Well, you've got a double, son. I don't know exactly where yet. But a double somewhere.' He winked and moved away to join his colleagues. 'It'll come to me.'

Grimm returned to his meal but his mind wasn't on it. This hadn't happened before and it worried him. Being close to the president, even for such a short time, meant he had been seen by a heap of people. And, in those circumstances, folk tended to remember faces. It might just be a matter of time before the senator remembered more precisely where he had seen his fellow guest. He gave the impression of being the kind of feller who didn't let things go. A bit like

Grimm himself in that respect.

For that reason it was a good thing that Grimm was planning to check out of the hotel. In fact, might be better if he got his hide completely out of town for a spell. Over a couple of weeks there was every chance he would run into the politician again if he stayed around. He went back to the law office.

'Hell, you're an eager beaver,' the marshal grinned, as his visitor heavy-footed through the door. 'Still ain't heard nothing. Said it'll take a couple of days.'

'Yeah, I understand. Ain't come about that. I was just wondering: while I'm here, mind if I have a look at your dodger file? Can't let the grass grow under my feet for too long. Gotta start thinking about my next job.'

'Sure thing. Anything to oblige.' The lawman opened a drawer and pulled out a small sheaf of reward posters and related documents. 'Not much I'm afraid but you're welcome to cast an eye over them.'

Grimm did so. The man was quite right. There weren't many there. And almost all of them were known to the bounty hunter – and had been passed over by him for lack of leads. 'That it?'

The lawman rooted through the drawer and pulled out a remaining paper which he looked over. 'Except for this one. But you wouldn't be interested in it. Bit of a blank. Ain't even got a picture on it.'

'Mind if I have a look?'

Grimm took the document and glanced over

it. Some hardcase wanted for murder. Winchy
Johnson. And, as the lawman had said, no
picture and no leads to speak of. Just a vague
description, the man's birthplace in Juarez and a
few more biographical details.

'On the button,' he concluded, handing the
paper back. 'Not a promising operation. Is that
it?'

'Yeah.'

'Looks like I'm gonna have to cut my suit
according to the cloth as my old ma used to say,'
the bounty hunter concluded, moving to the
door. 'I'll start by settling my tab at the hotel and
getting fixed up in one of the drovers' places.'

Outside, he paused at the boardwalk edge to
let an incoming stagecoach lurch past, then he
crossed the street to the hotel.

* * *

Some minutes later he was coming out of the
hotel with his saddle-bags over his shoulder. He
started heading along the boardwalk, not
relishing the prospect of having to lay his back
on a drover's palliasse, when the marshal hailed
him from across the street.

He crossed over and joined the lawman
outside his office.

'Stage has just come in,' the marshal said.

'Yeah. I saw it.'

'Brung in some'at that might be of interest to
you. Come inside.'

The bounty hunter followed him and closed

the door and took a screed off his desk. 'This was amongst the mail on the stage. Might be the kinda thing a guy in your line would be looking for if you're still fiddle-footed. But you'd have to move your butt.'

'What is it?'

'News in from Freshwater Creek; that's a town a spell back along the trail. Bank was knocked over yesterday. This communication from the marshal there is asking me to be on the look-out for a stranger coming though. Just one guy. There's his description.'

Grimm read it: average height, thinning ginger hair, couple of metal teeth; and he had been riding a pinto when he'd pulled the robbery.

'How do I fit in?'

'Figure the bank will be offering a reward. If you got a burr in your britches, you might want to follow this up instead of just kicking your heels round here in Constitution.'

Grimm thought about it. This was a possibility; could kill a couple of birds. It would save him from hanging around town while that politician was about the place scratching his head trying to figure where he'd seen Grimm; and it could bring in some cash. He gestured with the paper in his hand. 'If I took a crack at this, you'll put a hold on my Burdick money when it comes in?'

'Sure thing.'

Grimm nodded as he made the decision and walked over to a map on the wall. 'OK, where's this bozo heading?'

The lawman joined him and poked a thick finger at the map. 'That's where we are, Constitution. And there's Freshwater. According to the information the robber lit out of town on the northern trail. You head north-east from here you'll cut the north trail about here. That'll save you some riding and time.'

Grimm followed the finger and absorbed the geography. 'Thanks for the nod, Marshal. Figure I'll give it a whirl. One last thing: I'd be obliged if you would copy out the information you got on the case and sign it. It could help if I run into some legal authorities and I have to back up any heavy-handed action that I might take.'

THREE

The next morning he saddled up Burdick's horse and headed out of town on the trail leading to Freshwater. It would have been useful to call in at the law office of the town where the robbery had taken place in the hope of getting more information on the criminal; but time was of the essence so, following the marshal's directions, in advance he swung north-east to cut the northern trail out of Freshwater.

Once more alone in the saddle and with Constitution well behind him he had time to think. Like any other commercial enterprise, bounty hunting had its risks. First off, the operative had no way of knowing whether a job would take a week or six months. Time was money. It was the scarce resource that the operative invested in a project and he had no indication of how much was going to be needed. Second, villains were a varied bunch but one thing they had in common: none cottoned to looking the wrong way down a gun barrel. So, cornering a hardcase jumped up a guy's risk of getting his own head blown off. A head was a scarce resource too, seeing's he only had one.

Then, even if you pulled in a wanted hardcase in a fair time without getting your own skull ventilated, there was a third unknown quantity: the pay off. The figure printed on the reward poster was what a chaser could reasonably expect to get. If you were lucky and the villain had been active in the interim, the figure might even be raised as the paying agency – insurance or freight company, railroad or whatever – reappraised the value to their business of getting the owlhoot stopped.

But the prospect of reappraisal by the paying agency opened another possibility: downsizing the offered reward. Very, very rarely that happened. But it had happened with Whitey Burdick and the bounty hunter had to accept it. That was what was called taking the rough with the smooth.

*   *   *

Grimm had kept his eyes on the riders from the moment he had spotted them on the horizon. It was nearly noon – he figured by then he was quite a piece to the north of Freshwater – and the trail had become nothing more than a path of flattened grass splitting rolling meadowland of wild grasses. When the distant dots strung themselves out in single file he could count six. As they got yet closer he could see that each of them was heavily armed. That this was a posse was confirmed when sunlight glinted off a badge toted by the lead horseman. Grimm drew rein when the lawman up front raised his hand to halt his followers.

'Figure we might be on the same business,' Grimm said, leaning over his saddle horn when they met up.

'What might that be?' the lawman said.

'I'm told the fellow who robbed the bank in Freshwater was headed this way.'

'And you are?'

'Jonathan Grimm, bounty hunter.'

'Ain't see'd you in Freshwater.'

'No. I was in Constitution when the news came through. Marshal Berringer of that town gave me details. I cut across from there. Heard the desperado was heading north.'

The marshal nodded. 'Well, ain't seen hide nor hair of the critter. Mind, the varmint had a head start. We went as far as the county line. Ain't got the resources to go chasing beyond my jurisdiction. Anyways, the desperado could be anywheres now. I've wired all the local counties. It's up to them now, and the likes of you.' He threw a glance back at his fellow riders. 'My men have all got farms and businesses to get back to.'

Grimm dismounted and led his horse to one side to allow the group to pass along the narrow path.

'I wish you better luck than we've had,' the lawman said and gigged his horse. 'If you get your mitts on the bozo you know where to bring him.'

*   *   *

The sign said Big Springs. Grimm had seen
bigger but, for the region, it was a sizeable place
consisting of several streets which gridded the
weatherbeaten buildings into a number of
blocks. From what he had learned from the
posse lawman he reckoned he was now over the
county line.

It was late afternoon, not much travelling left
in the day. Besides he hadn't eaten since sun-up.
He saw to his horse then found himself a
restaurant. There was already one occupant, just
finishing his meal, an elderly guy with a headful
of snow-white hair.

Grimm threw him a howdy and the oldster
looked up with a face like some jovial gnome you
might see in a book of kid's fairy-tales. They
exchanged pleasantries and, as the newcomer
took a place near a window, a mother hen of a
woman came in from the kitchen to ask him his
requirements. He ordered a steak with all the
trappings and relaxed back in his chair to watch
the town go by through the glass while he waited.
Flatbed wagons passed. Bonneted women went
about their shopping. Across the street he saw a
trio of young drunks being tipped out from a
saloon by a barrel-chested barman. There was
some mouthing before the threesome recognized they were beat and resigned themselves to
sitting on the edge of the boardwalk.

Eventually the aproned woman brought him a
loaded plate and he attacked the vittles with

relish. After a spell the only other diner, the elderly man, finished his meal and paid his tab. The fellow's nankeen trousers and frock coat were crumpled. He set an equally sad-looking derby on his head and waddled towards the door, touching the hat in farewell to Grimm as he passed.

Grimm returned to his meal and would have paid the fellow no further mind but, glancing across the street a few minutes later, he saw the three juiced-up rowdies had circled him. There was some bantering and pushing. Then one flipped off the old man's derby and kicked him so that he went sprawling as he bent down to retrieve it.

It didn't take long for Grimm to ascertain the old guy had more than he could handle.

Grimm wiped a napkin across his greasy lips and stood up. One thing he didn't cotton to was the way some kids acted up these days. It was none of his business. On the other hand....

'Not to your liking, sir?' the old lady said from the kitchen, noticing his movement.

'Don't worry, ma'am,' he said. 'Ain't running out on the tab. Something's cropped up is all.'

She noted his half-finished meal. 'Shall I keep your plate warm?'

'Won't be that long, ma'am.' With that he pushed through the door and headed with a purposive gait across the main drag.

'All you have to do is give us a dance,' one of the rowdies was saying to the old man as Grimm got in earshot. 'Then you can be on your way.'

Grimm moved in front of the oldster and faced the rowdies. 'What gives?'

'Butt out, pilgrim,' one of the drunks slurred.

'This gent ain't here for your entertainment,' Grimm countered.

The old man touched Grimm's arm. 'I can look after myself, mister.'

'I know you can,' Grimm said. It was a lie; voicing it had something to do with leaving the oldster a tad of self-respect. 'Nevertheless, Grandpa, go about your business.' He gripped the old man, moved him aside and stepped back a pace so that he faced the three hotheads square on. 'These young men are going to see if they can make me dance instead. Ain't you, boys?'

The old man finally got a grip on his hat, then shuffled away, body swaying stiffly like a penguin.

'Now, fellers,' Grimm continued once the oldster was off the scene, 'what's all this bezazz about making folks dance? Some local custom or something?'

One of the men stepped back a pace and dropped his gun hand so that it hung near his holster. 'I've told you to butt out.'

The fingers of Grimm's hands flexed near the handles of his Army .44s. 'I'd like to see you go for that, kid. I real would.' His eyes flicked to the others. 'Your cronies are welcome to try their luck too. The more the merrier. Please.' His features were impassive so that an observer could guess nothing from them. But the slow deliberation in his tone told listeners he meant

what he said. It would take a no-brain to think that
a guy made such a challenge without knowing he
could back it up.

'Just joshing, mister,' one said, suddenly recog-
nizing the need for caution.

'Well, josh with me,' Grimm insisted. 'Ain't had
no fun today myself.'

'We ain't looking for trouble, mister.'

'Neither am I. And neither was that old guy.'

The foremost yahoo looked hard at the
stranger. Was difficult to tell his age. Tall, gaunt.
But ingrained powder marks on his cheekbone
indicated he had come out of at least one shooting
situation still on his feet. And the confident way
the hands lingered over his gun butts said that he
was no cupcake when it came to pulling iron.
Then there was the manner in which he had
butted in, prepared to take on three. Sober.

The youngster put out flattened hands to
placate his companions and said, 'We ain't making
nothing of it, mister.'

Grimm nodded. 'See, you can make a sensible
decision when you have to.' There was a scathing,
goading tone in his voice, as though he had got
the bit between his teeth and was loath to let the
thing set, even now that he'd crawfished them.

Tension still crackled but a voice said, 'Everybody cool it.' A figure was stepping forward and
stopped just short of interposing himself between
Grimm and the youngsters. 'This is the town
marshal,' he said, raising his hands.

'Sure thing, Marshal,' the lead troublemaker
said, and started backing away.

Grimm waited until it was plain the exchange had finished, threw a glance at the marshal then moved back towards the restaurant.

'I saw that,' the marshal said, walking alongside him. 'Youngsters got no jobs. Get juiced up and take it out on the world. Don't suppose a feller can blame 'em.'

Grimm kept on walking. 'In our day, you and me both had our problems, Marshal. But I figure, like me, you didn't take it out on an old guy like that. Ain't no excuse.'

'Yeah, you're right. Thanks for taking the oldster's part.'

'No thanks needed. I wouldn't have stepped in if I couldn't have handled them.'

'Anyways, anything I can do you for while you're in town, let me know.'

Grimm paused. 'There is one thing. I'm on the trail of a bozo, knocked over the bank in Freshwater.'

'You law?'

'No. Bounty chaser.' He took out the paper describing the robber and showed it the lawman. 'Forking a pinto. Not easy to miss him. Got a couple of metal teeth. Any stranger of that description rode in?'

The latter read the thing and shook his head. 'Not as I see'd. And I see most.'

'Much obliged, Marshal. Now if you'll excuse me, I got a meal getting cold.' And he pushed open the door back into the restaurant.

* * *

Big Springs had got its share of drinking parlours and during the evening Grimm made a tour on the look-out for his prey. In one saloon he saw the marshal again. In another he saw the three rowdies. They saw him but, now sobered up a mite, they gave him a wide berth.

In the fourth and last drinking house he saw no one with the metal teeth for which he was looking so he took a few relaxing shots of local hooch, then hit the hay.

Come sun-up he headed out.

FOUR

Grimm cleared pine and found himself looking down a slope at a small scatteration of buildings huddled round the trail. A one-hoss town if ever there was one. But he'd been riding all day so it was better than nothing. His chin bristling with dusty whiskers, he let his horse follow its head and made his way slowly down the grade.

There were no more than half a dozen wooden buildings and accompanying lean-tos. Up close he could hear noise coming from a shack and figured it served as a saloon. In the saddle since sun-up he itched for some liquid down his throat. He watered his horse, hitched it and stepped into the building that had caught his attention. It was a general store. In the middle a stove; on one side a counter backed by shelves containing assorted goods; on the other a rough-hewn bar with two characters seated round a glass-laden table.

'Howdy,' he said, standing in the doorway. They looked him over; he looked them over, watching their mouths as they grunted replies. No sign of metal teeth. More out-of-work waddies by all accounts, neither of them fitting the description in his pocket.

He bellied up to the bar as the proprietor, alerted by the voices, emerged from the back store-room.

'What's your pleasure, mister?' he asked, working lips dyed with tobacco juice.

Grimm ordered a beer, assuaged his thirst with a couple of swigs then moved over to a vacant chair.

'You travelled far, mister?' one of the others asked.

'Far enough.'

'Hope you ain't after work 'cos there ain't none.'

'Naw, just passing through.'

'That's the best thing to do with this place,' his companion added. 'Pass right on through.'

There was silence for a spell until one of the pair said, 'Mind, the place is sure getting busy. You're the second stranger to ride in today. More'n we usually get in a whole week.'

Grimm was interested. 'That so? This other guy, what's he look like?'

'Like any other bozo that's been on the trail a spell.'

'He got metal teeth?'

The other chuckled. 'Didn't make no close inspection. Only look in the mouth if it's woman or a hoss.'

Grimm went to the open door and looked around the hunch of shacks. His was the only horse on the street. And he'd already figured,

the place being so small, there was no other
drinking parlour around. He looked into the
distance at the trail fading under the evening sun
across the flat lands, then stepped back inside.
'This other feller, he carry right on through?
Can't see no hoss.'

'No. Last I saw he was headed for Myrtle's
place over the way. Her husband skedaddled so
she rents out a couple of bunks to make a buck.
Figure the stranger took one for the night.
Hosses are kept round back.'

'What kind of hoss he got?'

'Pinto.'

Pinto! Grimm nodded as he absorbed the
information. He had begun to think he was on a
wild goose chase, no sure idea where the bank
robber was heading, and only a written
description to go on. But now: a stranger had
ridden ahead of him into this God-forsaken
place. And on a pinto, too.

'He a sidekick of yours?' the fellow wanted to
know.

'Nope,' he replied, not wanting to disclose too
much of his business. 'But met up with a guy on
the trail aways back. Jus' wonder mebbe it's him.'

He finished his drink and headed out. As he
crossed the street he knew the fellow's eyes were
on him but it was of no concern. He passed the
frontage of the shack labelled Myrtle's, then
went round the back. There was a shack and
from it, an occasional hoof stomp. He investi-
gated and made out the unmistakeable pat-
terning of a pinto. Things were looking up. He

took out a gun, checked it was primed and returned it to its holster.

He walked round to the front again. After knocking he opened the door.

A woman was sitting knitting while a couple of kids played near a fire.

'You rent out bunks?' Grimm asked.

'Yes, sir. You want a place for the night?'

'Could be.'

She nodded her head to the door behind her. 'Got two in back.'

Grimm moved towards it. 'Can I have a look?'

The woman stood up. 'You'll have to be quiet. One bunk's been took already. Guy came in, real tired, asked not to be disturbed.'

Grimm pulled his gun and put his hand on the door handle.

'Hey, what is this?' the woman asked, putting her arms around the two children who, sensing a hard determination in their visitor, had scuttled over to her for protection.

Grimm raised a staying hand in her direction. 'Keep your voice down, lady. That way nobody gets harmed.'

He eased open the door, and light from the aperture fell on a bulky shape covered in a blanket. He stepped in, yanked back the blanket and thrust the gun at the sleeping head.

The head turned, bleary eyes opened. 'What in tarnation's going on?'

'Judas priest,' Grimm breathed. 'You again!' He did recognize the face, but there were no metal teeth. It was the old feller whose dignity he'd safeguarded back in Big Springs.

The oldster shuffled his body into a sitting position. 'Jehosophat, what a way to be woke up.'

'Sorry, pal. Thought you was somebody else.'

The old man rubbed his eyes, then spied the drawn gun. 'Well I'm sure glad I ain't somebody else.'

Grimm chuckled and sheathed his pistol. 'Hell, you sure get around some, mister. What you doing here?'

'You might have done me a good turn back in Big Springs, mister, but you don't own me. Don't have to tell you things.'

''Course you don't. Get yourself back to sleep. My apologies.'

Grimm got to the door but heard the fellow say, 'Can't sleep now. Not after being woke up like that. What time is it?'

'Around ten, give or take.' Grimm delayed closing the door, watching the man swing his legs off the bunk and rub his face into life. 'Listen, now I've woken you up, can I buy you a drink?'

'The night's still young.'

The fellow groped under the bunk for his boots. 'It'll be my call. I still owe you for muscling into that shindig at Big Springs.' When he had stomped into his footwear, he put out a hand. 'Name's Miller. Dwight Miller. Pleased to make your acquaintance.'

Grimm reciprocated and in a few minutes they were seated either side of a table in the general store with a couple of drinks between them.

'Fact is,' Grimm said when they had settled,

'I'm on the trail of somebody riding a pinto. Thought it was too much of a coincidence, another stranger coming through a backwater burg like this forking the same kind of bronc. How wrong can a guy be? I should have known better than to go off at half cock like that.'

The other considered the words as though they might mean something. 'Riding a pinto, eh? What's your angle?'

'Don't lose anything by telling you. This guy on the pinto: knocked over a bank in a place called Freshwater. I'm after his hide for the reward. I'm what some folks call a bounty-hunter. That's the way I make my money.' He grunted sardonically. 'Leastways that's the way it's supposed to work, only I seem to be losing the hang of it these days.'

The other nodded. 'This feller you got your sights on: ginger hair, couple of metal teeth?'

'On the button. How the hell do you know?'

'You talked about coincidences a minute back, Mr Grimm. I'll tell you what the coincidence is. I'm from Freshwater and the description you just reeled off is the one I gave to the marshal after the robbery. What's more I'm after the same feller.'

Grimm slapped his leg as he looked the oldster up and down. 'Hell, I see'd some bounty chasers in my time. They're a varied-looking bunch but, Jehosophat, you take the biscuit. Nobody would suspect you.'

'Naw, you got me wrong, Jonathan. I ain't one of them fellers.'

Grimm was even more perplexed. 'Well, how d'you mean: you're chasing him?'

'The way it fell, I was taking some money into the bank in Freshwater when this critter with a bandanna over his mush and a sixgun in his hand came busting in. Held up the bank, took what he could then, on the way out, grabbed my money too. A grand! When the dust had settled I asked the manager about my money and he said it was my loss. As I hadn't deposited it, it was nothing to do with the bank. I thought about it – it was all I had in the world – there was nothing else for me to do but light out after the feller myself.'

'How d'you know what he looked like? The metal teeth.'

'His bandanna slipped down as he was grabbing my cash.'

'Have you done this kind of thing before?'

'No. Used to run a drapery store in Freshwater. I'm getting on in years and figured it was about time I put myself out to grass, so I sold it. Got a good price too. Just collected the money and was in the act of depositing it. That's where the thousand came from.'

'And you're chasing an ornery desperado? Where's your gun?'

'Don't carry one.'

'How the bejesus would you tackle the critter if you catched up with him?'

'I'd work that out if and when I did catch up with him.'

Grimm grunted in disbelief. 'Hell, Mr Miller,

like as not this bozo's a hardened gun-toter. He'd blow you away!'

'Have to take that chance. The varmint's got all my worldly assets. Just ain't nothing else for me to do.'

Grim mused. The old guy had guts. But that was all he'd got. He pondered on it some more then came out with, 'OK, old-timer, here's the deal. I eat squareheads like this feller for breakfast. Only snag is I ain't got nothing more than a rough description in words of what he looks like. On the other hand, you've seen him face to face and can identify him. But, if you don't mind me saying, your chances of staying upright after a face-down with him are on a par with a snowball's chance in hell. Only one conclusion: you and me team up. You put the finger on him, I do the rest.'

'I'm in this to get my money back.'

'Ain't no guarantees. He might have stashed it away, or divvied it up with cronies. We both have to take our chances on what we get outa this.'

The oldster weighed it up as though there was a choice, then put out his hand. 'It's a deal, Mr Grimm.'

'OK, what else can you tell me about this spoiler?'

Miller parted his lips and touched his front teeth. 'Couple of metal teeth there. Not gold, tin, something like that. And a sharp-nosed face, you know, like some rodent.'

'Like a rat you mean?'

Miller nodded. 'Yeah. He's a rat all right.'

FIVE

Two days later they struck lucky. They'd pulled
into a place a good stretch over the county line.
Located at the crossroads of a couple of trails, it
was a big town. Although still afternoon the
place was already busy, the long hitching-racks
marking both sides of the main drag crowded
with horses, the saloons noisily full. It was clear
the settlement served as the focus of entertainment for the surrounding outfits.

After they had watered their horses at an old
log trough, Grimm stationed himself with a
drink in one parlour while Dwight checked out
the other establishments.

It wasn't long before the old waddy returned,
all fired up with excitement. 'He's here,
Jonathan. I've found him. Couldn't believe it.'

'Where?'

'Playing the wheel in one of the saloons along
the way. Cool as you like.'

'You sure it's him?'

'Sure as apples.'

Grimm downed his drink and indicated for his
companion to lead the way. The old man took

him along the sidewalk, then hesitated outside a pair of batwings and pointed. The sign above labelled it as a gaming establishment and the clamour of voices smothering a jangling piano indicated it was doing good business.

'Keep cool,' Grimm said. 'He doesn't know me and he probably won't recognize you if you keep out of the limelight. All you have to do is point him out. Then keep back and leave the rest to me.'

Inside, the long bar was virtually hidden by shoulder-to-shoulder drinkers. Under ribbons of smoke the rest of the place was thick on the ground with card and roulette tables.

'We'll take an easy drink,' Grimm said in a low voice. 'When you've pointed him out, I'll watch him for a spell. Wanna make sure the critter's got no sidekicks.'

'As far as I could see he pulled the job by hisself.'

'He might have met up with somebody. You never know.'

It took some time for them to get their hands round a couple of glasses, then they wormed their way through milling crowds, casually looking over poker and faro games.

Near a crowded roulette table Dwight paused and furtively pointed at the back of one of the players. Grimm gave a slight nod of his head to acknowledge receipt of the information, then indicated for the older man to continue along out of harm's way. The bounty hunter circled the table and stood watching from behind other onlookers.

With unsmiling slits for eyes, the guy stared impassively at the spinning wheel. The ginger hair and rodent features fitted the description given by Dwight. A glass and half-empty bottle of rye stood beside his chips. Judging by his breathing and the way his upper trunk swayed, he was on at least his second bottle.

There was a hush round the table as the ball clattered in the wheel. When it came to rest, a couple of guys cheered but the sneer given by rat-face indicated it was not a satisfactory result for him. The sneer showed something else too: a couple of metal teeth.

Grimm stayed that way for a few whirls of the wheel. During that time the fellow didn't speak to anybody. There was no space beside him and Grimm figured any buddy who had gone to the privy would have been back by now. Fairly sure the guy was a loner, he slowly worked his way round the table till he was behind him. The fellow clicked chips in his hand as he contemplated his next bet, unaware the bounty hunter was looking him over from the rear. The guy only carried one gun, a Smith and Wesson. For a quick draw, it was not thonged to the holster – but that served to Grimm's advantage too.

As the man leant forward once more to place chips on the betting grid, Grimm yanked the Smith and Wesson from its holster while simultaneously putting the barrel of his own gun in the man's back. 'Game's over. No funny business. This thing stuck in your kidneys is on a hair trigger.'

The man's hand moved instinctively to his side, only to encounter empty leather. He tried to turn but his boozed-up body was restricted by his sitting position and the proximity of Grimm.

The bounty hunter met the scattered voicings of alarm with, 'Don't worry, boys. All above board.' To his prisoner he said, 'Stand up and move from the table.'

'What's this all about?' the man said, rising ungainly.

Grimm said nothing and nudged him in the direction of the door. 'Cash his chips,' he said to Dwight, 'and meet up with us outside.' With that he began to manoeuvre the man towards the door, crowds parting in the suddenly hushed room.

He hadn't quite made it to the exit when another voice cut the air, an authoritative voice rasping, 'Just hold it there, mister.' A droop-shouldered fellow had extricated himself from the throng at the bar and advanced a couple of paces, enough for Grimm to see there was a gun in his hand and a badge on his chest. 'Town marshal,' the man declared. 'Explain yourself, mister.'

Grimm needed to restrict his prisoner while he handled the new development, so he pushed him to a chair clear of the door and commanded him to sit. 'And don't move.' Keeping his gun levelled he addressed the lawman. 'Bounty hunter, Marshal. Name of Grimm. Jonathan Grimm. Apprehending suspected fugitive. Robbed a bank in Freshwater.'

'You got the wrong fellow, Grimm,' the seated man growled.

'Oh no he hasn't,' Dwight put in. 'I've trailed him all the way from the scene of the robbery, Marshal. I'm a witness to the crime. And I'm testifying to the fact when we get the critter's hide to court.'

'And who are you?' the marshal wanted to know.

Dwight gave his particulars. The marshal looked around at the onlookers craning their necks, then said, 'Come over to my office, the three of you. We'll talk this thing out over there.'

In the quiet of the lawman's quarters Grimm explained the situation in more detail to the marshal and his deputy.

'You got a poster on this man?' the lawman wanted to know.

'No, sir.'

'No,' the prisoner butted in. 'And you don't even know my name. Hell, he can't go around arresting folk without naming 'em, can he, Marshal?'

'What's your name?' the marshal asked.

'Warren Tyler, sir.'

'And what you doing here?'

'Just riding through, sir. Minding my own business. Stopped off for some refreshment and some relaxation at the gaming tables is all.'

Grimm ignored the conversation and groped around in his pocket, fetching out a paper which he handed to the marshal. 'Got a description of the thief signed by a marshal by the name of Berringer. Not exactly a court order but it'll corroborate what we say.'

The badge man looked it over and nodded in recognition. 'I know Berringer. But he's marshal down at Constitution. What's he got to do with this caper?'

'That's where I was when the message came through,' Grimm explained.

'And what's the lawmen at Freshwater doing about it?'

'Posse gave chase out of Freshwater but stopped at the county line. I met 'em on the way back. They'd already got a message through to Constitution. Marshal said they were gonna circulate the details to other law agencies.'

The marshal shook his head. 'Well, nothing's come through yet.' He read the message once again and then returned the paper. 'Ain't much of a description but what there is fits. Ain't much mistaking them ugly teeth.'

'That's him all right, Marshal,' Dwight said. 'I positively identify him.'

The lawman looked at the three of them then said, 'Time for spot judgements. I figure you're on the square, Mr Grimm.'

'In that case, I'd be obliged if you could do me a favour, Marshal.'

'Go on.'

'This guy got away with a few thousand bucks.'

'A grand of which was mine,' Dwight interjected.

Grimm went on. 'Could you put the renegade in the slammer while I get his things together and go through them?'

'That's more a job for me,' the marshal said. 'I'll put the man in the cell and leave you here with my deputy while I find out where he's bunked.'

*   *   *

During his boss's absence the deputy treated them to coffee. Grimm took the opportunity to go through the fugitive's pockets, dredging up around a hundred dollars. He placed the bills and coins on the desk alongside the fifty dollars from the chips that Dwight had cashed.

It was some twenty minutes later when the lawman returned. He dumped a couple of saddle-bags on the desk. 'Zilch,' he said.

Grimm poked in the bags then looked towards the cell. 'The critter's stashed it someplace. I'll get it out of him.'

The lawman shook his head. 'No. I've been round the gaming parlours. Our friend stood out as a big better. The proprietors have kept tabs on him while he's been in town. They can't be exact but seems he managed to get through around three grand in two days.'

Grimm whistled. 'Can't we collect it off them?'

The lawman shook his head. 'Legitimately placed bets. They weren't to know it was stolen money. In fact it has to stand as legitimate until a court proves otherwise.'

Grimm looked at the sorry pile of cash on the desk. 'Judas Priest, so all we can take back is a hundred and fifty dollars?'

'You can't even take that,' the marshal said. 'I'm sticking that in my safe until the county judge tells me what to do with it.'

Dwight slumped into a chair. 'Does that mean I don't get a penny of my money back at all?'

'Looks that way,' the marshal said.

'Ain't as bad as that, Dwight' Grimm said. 'I couldn't have caught him without you. We're in this together and when we get the knucklehead back to Freshwater we split the bounty fifty-fifty. So you'll get something back, old pard.'

SIX

Figures watched solemnly from the sidewalks as the three riders passed down the main street of Freshwater.

'Recognize me, Marshal?' Grimm said as he heavy-footed into the law office. 'Name of Grimm. We met out on the trail. You said I knew where to come if I caught your bank robber. Me and your Mr Miller here, we done just that.'

Amazement was writ large on the lawman's features. 'You got him? Where?'

Grimm thumbed backwards. 'Awaiting your pleasure out on the drag. All in one piece too.'

The marshal led them back to the door and surveyed the scowling owl-hoot. 'I can't say how grateful we are, Mr Grimm.'

'Any need for gratitude don't get a look-in,' the bounty hunter said, looking down the street. 'Just accompany us to the bank so Mr Miller and I can pick up the reward. Any idea what it stands at?'

'Ah,' the other said, hanging on to the sound in a manner that created an unease in the bounty hunter.

Grimm looked at the marshal's face and knew

his unease was justified, seeing hesitancy stamped all over it. 'There's some kind of problem, Marshal?' he prompted.

'Better step back inside, Mr Grimm.'

The bounty hunter didn't move. 'What's the hitch?'

'Fact is, there's no reward. The bank's gone into liquidation.'

'Liquidation?'

'Yeah. Wasn't insured. Couldn't take the loss.'

'Judas Priest,' Grimm hissed, throwing a glance at his crestfallen companion.

'Take a walk and see for yourself,' the lawman went on. 'Place's all boarded up. Bank's ceased trading.'

Grimm thought about it. 'You got an address? There must be a head office.'

'Naw. It was a one-branch outfit.'

'Well, there must be fittings and things in the place that'll fetch a few dollars. Me and Miller here, we put a passel of effort into catching that *hombre*. We're entitled to something.'

'Can't be touched. The judge has put the whole place in escrow. There's a lotta local folk been hurt by this thing. They'll all be wanting a cut of whatever can be salvaged. Once it's been sold and the finances divvied up, won't work out at much more than a few dollars each. How much of the loot did you manage to retrieve?'

Grimm grunted. 'Would you believe the bozo hazarded the whole caboodle in gaming parlours and lost it? All he'd got on him was a hundred and fifty dollars.'

The marshal put out his hand. 'I'll have to ask you for that, Mr Grimm.'

'Can't oblige. Marshal of Big Springs took it, pending the case.'

The lawman shook his head. 'A pig's ass all round.'

'You don't know the half of it,' Grimm rejoined. 'This is the second time this has happened to me in a week.'

'Funny, ain't it?' the lawman mused. 'A bank going bankrupt.'

'Ain't all that funny,' the bounty hunter grunted.

'Sorry. Didn't mean it in that way. Just that you don't expect banks to run out of money. I mean, if banks ain't got money to meet eventualities, who has?'

Grimm was unconcerned with the philosophical fineries. 'So where's our payment coming from?'

'It just don't.'

The word 'Shoot' escaped from Grimm's lips. then he nodded back at the law office door. 'Do me a favour. Have a look through your files. See if anybody else is offering a reward for him. The bank heist could be just the latest of a string of his crimes. Might be somebody else benefiting from his being put out of action and prepared to pay for it.'

'You get a name out of him?'

'Said his name is Warren Tyler.'

The marshal took them into his office and pulled open a drawer, extracting a wad of papers. He flicked through them, passing them to Grimm in turn.

'I'm sorry, Mr Grimm,' he concluded. 'As you can see, if any other agencies are offering a reward I don't have a record of it.'

'Seems there ain't much point hanging about here no longer,' Dwight Miller chipped in. 'I'm gonna have to get home to my missus. She'll be fretting about me. And you're coming with me, Mr Grimm. Like me, you must be starving.'

They all moved outside and Grimm raised his hands in a supplicant manner in the direction of the outlaw who was still astride his horse. 'Marshal, the hardcase is all yours.'

*   *   *

Mrs Miller was more concerned to see her husband return without harm than the fact that the money hadn't been recovered. She was a homey old gal and was soon airing blankets in preparation for Grimm stopping over.

She cooked well too and, after a filling meal, the two men took a smoke on the porch.

'So what kind of a spot are you really in?' Grimm asked when he'd ensured Mrs Miller was out of earshot.

'Oh, we'll manage.'

'Don't give me that "we'll manage" crud. You and I have rode a hard trail together. We know enough about each other to be a mite more open than that. Was the money Tyler took all you'd got?'

The oldster breathed deep. 'Most of it. See, we rent this place. Mrs Miller and me, we ain't as young as we used to be. I'd been running the drapery store in town. We'd worked out the figures and decided it was about time for me to retire. So we sold it as a going concern. Got a grand. Then my intention was to buy this place so that we could spend our last days without working quite as hard as we've been used to. All seemed to be working out well. The landlord wants far less than a grand for this place so I'd have some over. We grow most of our own stuff. Mebbe I could do a bit of part-time work if we needed luxuries now and again. So things seemed to be working out OK. That is, till that ugly sidewinder stepped into the Freshwater bank and spoiled everything.'

'What you aim to do now?'

'Rent's paid up till the end of the month. I got enough to stretch another couple of months. Give me time to think what to do next. Suppose I could start working again. Must say, it'd stick in my craw to be employed in the very store I used to own. But who's gonna take on a creaking old bozo like me anyhows?'

'Well, I'll get out of your hair tomorrow. Can't afford to feed me as well.'

'Jonathan, you stay as long as you like. You're our guest.'

The two tired men finished their smokes then turned in.

* * *

The next morning Miller directed Grimm to the telegraph office so that he could wire the marshal at Constitution. The reply soon came back: still no news on the Burdick bounty.

At that point, acutely aware of being an additional burden on the old folk, Grimm wanted to leave but the old man insisted he stay on, at least until he got a positive wire.

But the next day it was still the same. Mid-morning they were standing on the boardwalk outside the telegraph office with Grimm looking at yet another dud reply from Constitution.

'The hell with this,' he said, 'I'm having a drink. Come on, Dwight.'

As they walked towards the nearest saloon they passed some local government building just as a figure stepped out on to the boardwalk.

'We meet again.' It was a loud voice, clearly enunciated by someone used to public speaking. Grimm hadn't seen the fellow but looked sideways and recognized him immediately. Hell's teeth, the politician from Constitution.

Grimm flicked a finger in acknowledgement and carried on walking.

'Washington,' the man declared loudly at their rear. 'I'm sure of it now.'

Grimm paused, turned and forced a smile. 'Sorry, pilgrim. Like I've told you before, never been that far East.'

'It's coming. I'm sure it was somewhere in Washington. Different clothes, different situation, but everything about you is unmistakable.

You got a certain way of moving. I've seen you before, feller.'

Grimm remembered an old saying of his ma's: it never rains but it pours. Then an expletive came to his mind of which his ma would not have approved. Ignoring the politician who was still looking at him quizzically, he pushed through the batwings.

'Who is that guy?' he asked Miller, when they were settled with a drink.

'Used to be our congressman in Washington. Lost his seat. Now he's in local politics.'

'He sure gets around.'

'Lives here in town, but spends time at the county seat in Constitution. You stay in these parts you'll see more of him.'

That was something Grimm didn't cotton to. The way the mandarin's mind was ticking over, it wouldn't be long before he firmed up exactly where and when he'd seen Grimm. The sooner the bounty hunter got the hell away from Freshwater and Constitution the better. He'd calculated that taking time out to chase after Tyler would have solved his problem. But it wasn't enough. He needed to put a whole passel of miles between himself and the politician – permanently. But he couldn't cut loose, not just like that. His horse back in Constitution needed its mending time; not to mention the matter of a bounty supposed to be coming through. It was small but the way things had been falling he needed every dollar he could get his hands on.

What he needed was to get right out of the

locality for a few weeks. He knew his steed was in good hands. He trusted Andy at the livery. And Marshal Berringer had promised to hang on to his money when it came. But he needed money now.

Then he had the idea. A way of getting out of the limelight and with a purpose of its own. Two birds with one stone. He cast his mind back to Berringer's dodger file. There'd been a case there, unpromising at the time and he'd dismissed it.

But it was a prerequisite in his line of country that he had an efficient memory. He called up the details from the back of his mind. Winchy Johnson, that was the name. The nickname stemmed from the hardcase's preferred weapon: the reading had said he was a capable man with a Winchester. Wanted for murder in Denver. Reward: $3000.

Three grand. That would solve his present difficulties. Including a slice for Dwight. The oldster was a regular guy and it would be good to throw some dinero his way. He had helped the bounty chaser, even though it had been an abortive escapade. And now, despite his world collapsing around him like a house of cards, the old-timer and his good wife were prepared to offer Grimm hospitality as long as he wanted it.

He threw his mind back and focused on what he could recall of the wanted man's description: slightly above average height, mouse-coloured hair. Born in Juarez of Anglo father, Mexican mother. So, he'd be looking for a 'breed. Not much to go on, except one thing that had stood out when he had originally read it: the fellow had had part of his face shot away which had left a massive scar on his right cheek, an injury which hampered his speech. Shouldn't be difficult to identify him – if a feller should ever catch up with him. Ay, there was the rub.

From what he remembered, the record said he'd gone to earth and hadn't been sighted for over six months. Only one thing for it. Start at Juarez. A guy goes missing for a long spell, returning to his roots was a bet. Not a dead cert, but enough of a possibility to put it in the field.

Snag with that, it was in Mexico and a hunter could have trouble with the authorities if there was a shoot-out. Didn't matter what country, badge-toters didn't cotton to foreigners coming in and throwing lead around. Not to mention the problem he could have in getting his man over the border. But that bridge was a long way away.

He mulled it over. It was a long shot but it would keep him out the area for a spell, long enough for his horse's leg to heal. The more he thought about it the more it appealed.

'You're quiet, my friend,' Dwight said.

'Just thinking through my options.'

Before they had left the saloon he had made a firm decision and informed his companion that he was lighting out at sun-up.

Mexico, here I come.

SEVEN

He thought the scrawny dog was dead, lying as it was, immobile on its side in the middle of the thoroughfare, oblivious to the occasional traffic ambling on either side of it. As he neared he saw the mutt's ribcage moving. Closer, it monitored his passing with a half-opened eye. It wasn't dead. It just felt like he did.

So this was Cuidad Juarez, gateway to Mexico. Or gateway to the U.S., according to which way a guy was headed. In appearance not too different from a whole passel of towns in Texas. As it should be, given that the Lone Star state – with which he had more than a tad of familiarity – had once been under the Mexican tricolour.

A long journey like the one he had undertaken all the way from Freshwater USA needed two horses so he had commandeered Tyler's. Alternating the two, it had taken him five days to reach the Rio Grande. Tyler's mount had been a mite uppity but there was compensation that Burdick had known his horseflesh and had forked a good steed. One out of two wasn't bad.

He had dismounted and crossed one of the

two bridges that linked the northern territory of
Mexico with El Paso. Both crossovers were heavy
with traffic, watched over by US and Mexican
officials who only occasionally stopped a traveller
to break the tedium of swatting flies as they
leaned against an adobe wall.

Beyond the bridge he had stopped to count his
money. Reminding himself yet again of the need
to watch his pennies, he had resumed his walk
past the famous Guadelupe Mission; then past
cantinas, women flip-flapping tortillas under
porches that looked ready to collapse; past
slumbering *peons* under sombreros. He had
guided his tired horses around oxen, mules and
sheep until the substantial streets and plazas
became dirt tracks.

In the search for cheap lodgings he continued
to the outer part of town and wasn't disappoin-
ted. He found a cantina that could provide him
with a cot at a price that wouldn't put him on
Poverty Row before he'd even started his
investigations. It was a border town so his US
currency was acceptable, in fact preferable. And
his time in Texas had given him enough of the
Spanish lingo to get by. After the long, slow
journey south his main concern for himself and
animals was food and rest; and this he arranged
for cents that would have bought him no more
than a couple of drinks over the river.

*   *   *

The next morning after breakfast he took a stroll

through the town. He passed the imposing court building on a main boulevard and noted the location of the *federale* station. He passed a commercial building. Through the high open doorway he could see traders bartering over samples of cotton. Given the babbling humanity in there and the amount of merchandise he guessed the town had to be some kind of central market for the region's cotton business.

He moved on and pushed through the batwings of a cantina bearing the unmerited name of 'Paradiso'. Someone was strumming a guitar and a bearded swamper was sweeping the floor. Grimm advanced to the bar and leaned an elbow on the flat surface. There was no one behind it and he looked around for service.

A fat man seated at a card table looked up. 'Hey, Julio. Serve the gentleman. I got a good hand here.'

The swamper leant his brush against the bar. He said something in Spanish which Grimm didn't understand, then put up 'Gringo, eh?' for confirmation.

'*Sí.*'

'OK, Gringo, what can I get for you?' the swamper continued in an English which was almost as unintelligible as his Spanish.

Grimm looked at the stained teeth smiling at him through the unkempt beard, the dirty fingernails on the end of grimy hands, and quickly concluded that he didn't want anything that this bozo put his mitts on; but he settled for 'A glass of beer, *por favore.*'

He heavy-footed across the planking with the beer and sat at a table. For a while he took stock of the place, absorbed the atmosphere, then set to thinking.

Where was the best place to start making enquiries in a strange town? Over a drink in a saloon was always a good start. The card-playing cantina owner maybe? The swamper would be a good bet. That kind picked up all the town scuttlebutt and would be willing to provide information for cents. But he didn't want to get pegged as a snoop on his first day in town.

Where else, who else? There was the federale building. It was their business to know things. They might come up with something for him. But they would want to know his reasons. If ever he caught up with this Winchy Johnson he would have to break Mexican law to get him out. He could spin them some tale about the reasons for his search but, again, he would be drawing attention to himself at an early stage. That was discounted too.

Who was likely to know things and keep stum? He was half way down his beer when he heard the bells of the Mission calling the faithful. That was it. What a priest didn't know about a town usually wasn't worth knowing. And a man of the cloth wasn't likely to go blabbing about a guy asking questions.

He downed his drink and with an 'Adios' pushed through the batwings into the harsh glare of the sun.

In the distance he could see the white tower of

the Mission that he had passed with hardly a glance on his entry the previous day. He made his way in its direction and stood in the plaza looking up at it, and at the worshippers shuffling up the steps. It was plain to the urchins milling around that he was a visiting gringo and they began to jostle him with their hands extended. Huh, the poor kids were on to a bum steer with him. He had hardly enough dinero to sustain himself, never mind subsidising the town's overpopulation.

'*Vamos*,' he grunted, drawing on his basic Spanish vocabulary. Even so he had to repeat it with more aggression before they did so. One lingered looking at him. 'You're interested in the Mission of Nuestra Señora de Guadelupe, *señor*? She fine Mexican building built in 1659.' His English was faltering but it came out mechanically and it was clear the young kid was used to giving Americano visitors what they wanted to hear.

Grimm didn't dismiss him so the boy continued at a respectful distance. 'It is called Guadelupe, *señor*, for the reason that there was a shepherd in Guadelupe in Spain many years ago; he found an image of Our Lady that had been hidden by the Moors. Back in the old country the mission became a place of pilgrimage. And now, *señor*, we have our own Guadelupe, here in Mexico. In our own Juarez. We are so proud.'

Grimm wasn't interested in the spiel but he liked the kid. And he might be useful sometime. 'What's your name, kid?'

'Ricardo, *señor.*'

Grimm flicked him a shining dollar. 'Ricardo, you got some persistence. I'll give you that. *Gracias.*' With that he joined the throng going up the steps.

Rubbing shoulders with the devotees, he felt awkward. He wasn't a Catholic, wasn't sure what to do, so he imitated the others making the sign of the cross as he entered.

Inside he took a pew at the back and followed the motions of the rest of the congregation. At the conclusion of the mass he waited till the bulk of the worshippers had filed up the aisle to leave, then he went to the side of the building and moved towards the front. The priest was standing watching his departing flock.

'Excuse me, Father,' Grimm said.

'Yes, my son?'

'I wonder if you can help me. I am trying to trace a man who was born in Juarez.'

'I will help if I can. What is his name?'

'Frank Johnson. Or rather Francisco. That was his church name. Born of an American father and Mexican mother.'

The priest ran the name round his mind. 'Francisco Johnson? No. I think I would have remembered such a name. Why do you seek him?'

'I just happen to be passing through your beautiful city and a friend of Frank's asked me to look him up while I was here.'

'I'm afraid I cannot help. Perhaps I suggest that you make enquiries at the government office. He should be on the electoral roll.'

Grimm doubted it but he said, 'Good idea. *Gracias, Padre.*'

As he walked towards the front entrance a man stepped from behind a pillar and touched his arm. He was dressed in the manner of an affluent *vaquero*, shiny conchos decorating his leggings. 'I overheard your words with the priest, *señor*,' he whispered. 'I can help you in your search.' He looked about furtively. 'But we cannot talk here. If you want to hear what I have to say, be at the rear of the Casa del Aguila at sun-down.'

'Can't you tell me anything before then?'

The man backed off, patting the air with flattened hands. 'The Casa del Aguila at sun-down. *Por favore, señor*, be patient.' With that the man turned and strode briskly out of the church.

Grimm watched the man depart then strolled towards the exit. Getting to the sunlight streaming in through the front doorway, he was just in time to see the man board an elegant buggy. The man dropped on to a seat alongside a black-veiled woman and flicked the ribbons.

Grimm sat on a step and watched the buggy disappear. He pondered on the quickness of the exchange. Had the man seen someone watching or was he being naturally cautious in not wanting to talk there and then? After all, it would be just a matter of passing on some details and, presumably, being paid for the information. Whatever the reason for the subterfuge it was a lead he had to follow up. But, with his horses quartered at the rooming-house and needing rest, he couldn't follow the buggy; nothing for it but to leave his questionings till the promised meeting.

He suddenly became aware of a small shape sitting on the step behind him. He turned and recognized the grinning teeth that belonged to the street urchin he had met earlier.

'Hey, Ricardo,' he said. 'Did you see the buggy with the *señor* and *señorita*? The one that just left.' He pointed in the direction.

'*Si, señor.*'

'You know who they were?'

'There are not many in Juarez that Ricardo does not know, *señor*.'

'Well?'

A grimy hand was extended.

Grimm grunted, fished through his pockets, and dropped a dollar into the waiting palm.

'The *señora* is Consuela Maria Galinas de Zedari. Sister to Don Ruiz Galinas de Zedari.'

Grimm nodded. 'And the gentleman who accompanied her?'

The now empty hand came out once again.

'There was a time when I thought I'd got a good racket, kid,' the bounty hunter said, 'but the way my luck's been running and watching you operate I'm beginning to have my doubts.' And he refilled the hand.

'Carlos Medillo, *segundo* to Don Ruiz Galinas de Zedari.'

Without prompting, Grimm put another dollar in the kid's hand. 'And you can tell me where they live, *muchacho*?'

'Rancho Libertad, *señor*. About five miles

south-east out of town.'

By this time Grimm had lost track of the mouthful of Spanish names he had been given earlier so he asked for a repeat, which surprisingly he got free of charge.

*   *   *

The last rays of the sun were shimmering on the Rio Grande as he made his way along smelly mule-tracks. The Casa del Aguila was a cantina at the other end of town. He didn't think there could be a more decrepit area than where he was lodging, but he was wrong. This place was a couple of pegs down on that. Manure heaps spilled into the thoroughfares and hardened chickens challenged a traveller's passage. Here and there were voices, the sound of a baby crying.

The façade of the cantina was poorly lit and he could just make out a crudely painted Eagle above the door. He made his way down the dark alleyway at the side of the adobe. Of all the places for an assignation with a stranger in a foreign country.

There was a narrow alleyway at the back and, judging by its stench, the building across the way was a privy. He looked up and down, confirmed the *vaquero* wasn't there yet, and took out his pipe and tobacco pouch. If he was going to spend much time in the spot he would at least try to blanket the smell with the aroma of some honest Virginian. After he had lit up he leant against the wall and waited. A couple of sombreroed Mexicans passed, chattering and laughing. He watched them until they had disappeared round a corner at the far end, then he resumed his vigil.

After he had smoked half a bowl, during which he observed many other revellers pass to and fro, he came to the conclusion he was wasting his time. Not that he had anything else more pressing to do but the smells were getting to him. He gave the mysterious Carlos another five minutes, then headed back to his lodgings.

EIGHT

The next day he rode out to the Rancho Libertad with the intention of seeing what he could turn up on the *segundo* Carlos. As he journeyed south, the cacti-dotted scrubland greened up a little and eventually he came across bunches of grazing cattle. Not the large Texas longhorns with which he was familiar but their smaller cousins, black sharp-horned cimarrones, bred from the mustang cattle of mesquite country. As he progressed their number increased indicating he was on the Don's spread. He topped a rise and paused to look down. There was a single-storeyed house built in the Spanish style, surrounded by an assortment of outbuildings and corrals. That had to be the rancho. He was taking in the scene when a couple of riders came up behind him.

In Spanish they questioned him as to his business on Libertad land. There was a hardness in their manner: as they rested in the saddle, he recognized the posture of their hands which, seemingly drooped casually, gave clear passage to their gun butts. They were looking for some action. He concluded that to pass them off with

71

some story that he was just drifting through could give them their excuse. Had they been side by side he could probably have handled them, even if they drew first, but they had been careful enough to position themselves as split targets.

So he said, 'I wish to see the *segundo, señor* Medilla.'

They looked at each other and one said, 'Oh, you do, eh? You better come with us, *señor.*'

He was escorted down the slope, past whitewashed adobe walls and fences and into the domestic compound. He dismounted and hitched his horse at a rail underneath an exotically-leaved tree.

'You stay here, *señor,*' one said and crossed the patio. At the door of the hacienda the man took off his sombrero and spoke with someone. There was a delay of some minutes, then Grimm was beckoned over.

There was an aged *mestizo* lady at the door. 'If you will follow me, *señor.*' Grimm took off his hat and complied. The floors were polished to a mirror finish and resounded to the clatter of his boots. He was shown to a large sitting-room which had two occupants: the woman he had seen in the buggy in Juarez and an elderly man. A family resemblance was noticeable between them. Now without her veils, the woman revealed herself to be attractively featured, around thirty. The well-sculpted head of the man with its similar straight-cut features gave him a patrician's air.

Grimm quickly took in the room: the patterned

blankets hanging from the adobe walls, the heavy Spanish furniture. the statues on mantels.

In ornately decorated bolero and leggings, the elderly man rose and advanced a few paces towards the visitor. 'I am Don Ruiz Galinas and this is my sister Consuela.'

Grimm responded with his own name and nodded in the direction of the woman and man in turn. 'Honoured to make your acquaintance, *señorita*. And you, *señor*.'

'Yes, indeed.' The man swung a hand indicating the pleasantries were now over. 'You seek my *segundo*, *señor*. You know him?'

'No, *señor*.'

'Then what business do you have with him?'.

'I am in need of work and I am told he might be able to offer me some.'

'I don't know who told you that, *señor*. We run, how do you say, a very tight ship here at the Libertad. We only employ tried and trusted workers. Thus we retain a loyal complement. There is rarely opportunity for outsiders. Besides, there have always been many men in Chihuahua who have no work and are willing to labour for a wage far lower than any gringo would expect.'

'Oh, I see.'

'What kind of work would you seek?'

'Any kind.'

'I think not, *señor*. You do not carry the hands of a *vaquero*.'

Grimm needed to change the topic. 'Is there any chance of me seeing *señor* Carlos?'

'That is not possible. He is absent from the

rancho on business. Besides, as I have said, there is no opportunity for work so there is nothing to be gained from seeing him.'

'In that case, I will thank you for your time and bid you good day.'

'Where are you staying?' The bleak formality had now left the *ranchero*'s voice.

'In Juarez.'

'That is a long ride. Will you take some refreshment with us before you go?'

'That is kind, *señor*.'

'I am just about to sample a wine that has recently arrived from Spain. You may wish to join me in a glass.' The man called and the *mestizo* woman shuffled in. He gave instruction and shortly she returned with a bottle. She took expensive crystal glasses from a cabinet while the *ranchero* uncorked the bottle.

'I can tell by your speech that you have not been in Mexico long,' the man said after Grimm had complimented him on the full-bodied red wine from which he had taken a considered sip. 'Nevertheless, you speak passable Spanish for an Anglo.'

'I spent some time in Texas, *señor*.'

'Doing what?'

Grimm had come to get some questions answered but was getting the grilling himself; however he saw no harm in letting the *hidalgo* know something. 'I put my hand to many things. For a time had my own spread.'

'And what stock did you work?'

'Horses.'

The man nodded. 'But that was a long time ago.

What labour has occupied those fingers since?'

'This and that,' Grimm said, finishing his wine. Realizing that he was wasting his time and was not going to see the *segundo* or learn anything about him, he said, 'Well, thank you for your hospitality, *señor*, but I must be going.'

Farewells were exchanged and Grimm made his way outside. Consuela crossed to the window. She watched the visitor mount up and ride up the gentle slope. 'I am worried, Ruiz. As you said, that man is not a ranch-hand. I do not understand why such a stranger should come asking after Carlos at this time?'

'Do not worry, my dear sister. I have paid Carlos off. He was becoming a nuisance. He didn't hide his infatuation for you. He should have known the sister of an *hidalgo* would have no truck with a common workman.'

'He was harmless. And I did nothing to encourage him.'

'My dear. His besottedness was such that your merest glance was enough to feed him for days.' He stood behind her and gripped her shoulders. 'But it is past. Even Carlos could be bought off with a big enough sum. There is nothing to worry over now.'

* * *

The following morning Grimm was contemplating his next course of action. The fact that the man called Carlos had asked to see him strongly suggested he wasn't on a wild goose chase down

here in Juarez. It was just a pity that the man
hadn't been able to make the rendezvous. Something must have cropped up to prevent him being
in Juarez that evening. The guy was a *segundo* on a
big rancho. He would have responsibilities and
tasks to do. Maybe the man would contact him on
his return, from wherever he had gone.

Stymied for the moment, the bounty hunter
would let things roll a spell and see if anything
developed. There would be no harm in hanging
around and familiarizing himself with the town.

He washed, shaved and had breakfast. After
seeing to the horses he took a mosey round the
town. He found a cantina where he watched the
world go by over a drink. He watched the ox carts
laden with cotton bales winding through the
town. Saw the urchins begging round the Guadalupe Mission.

Back at his lodgings in the afternoon the
landlady was waiting for him.

'There is a message for you, *señor*,' she said,
handing him a piece of paper.

'Who delivered it?' he asked as he unfolded the
missive.

The woman shrugged and pulled a wry face. 'A
peon. Do not know his name. Never saw him
before. He left very quickly. As soon as the note
was in my hand. Just said you would understand.'

Grimm looked at the words crudely scrawled in
capital letters: 'My apologies for not making our
meeting. Will see you same place, same time
tonight.' It ended with an enigmatic C. Had to be
Carlos.

'The fellow who delivered this, what did he look like? Did he have the appearance of a *vaquero*?'

She chuckled. 'No, *señor*. Not a *vaquero*. Moth-eaten poncho. Straw sombrero that was falling apart. Just like a thousand other *peons*.'

Wasn't Carlos himself. That was clear. Some nonentity paid to deliver a message was all. He looked again at the reverse side of the paper. It bore his name: Sr Grimm. That raised a point: how would this Carlos know his name? He'd only met the fellow once, casually in the church. This was getting more intriguing.

With a '*Gracias, señora*' he repaired to his room to wait for nightfall.

* * *

Once again he made his way to the Casa del Aguila and walked along the now familiar alleyway alongside the building. It was almost pitch-black when he got to the back but he could see enough to see there was no one there. Yet again. Maybe he was too early. He slowly walked up and down, his eyes and ears alert, the smell of urine and other unpleasant odours strong in his nostrils. Suddenly his boot hit something. He looked down to see a shape. There was somebody bunched up on the ground. The figure was definitely still and hadn't been disturbed by his tripping against it. He knelt down. It was too dark to make any investigation. Probably some drunk. None of his business, that was for sure.

As he rose a voice rasped down the alley behind him. 'Put up your hands, *señor*, then, do not move.'

A few seconds later there was a policeman beside him, pistol levelled. He felt his guns being taken, then a voice: 'What have we here, *señor*?' as a boot kicked the shape on the ground.

Grimm shrugged in the darkness. 'Don't know. Guess that's a drunk down there.'

'You don't know, eh? *Anda*! Let us have a look. Alonso, get a lamp from the cantina. And you …' – the gun barrel poked in Grimm's ribs – 'step back against the wall.' As he complied he could see there were three officers besides the one giving orders. One disappeared inside the cantina while the other two covered him as he stood backed against flaking adobe.

The kerosene that was brought enabled a closer inspection to be made. Grimm had had only had a short exchange with Carlos in the church but the oil lamp threw enough light for him to recognize the *vaquero*.

'This *hombre* is dead,' the leading policeman said, loudly and matter-of-factly as he returned to a standing position. 'And you don't know anything? *Vaya*!'

Grimm pointed to his weapons in the grip of an officer. 'You check those guns your man has taken off me, you'll see they haven't been fired.'

The policeman laughed. 'What are you talking about? You don't need guns to slit a man's throat. You're going to headquarters, *amigo*. Now get moving.'

NINE

His uniform stained and sweat-circled around the armpits, the policeman was perched on the corner of a desk, swinging one of his legs as he looked at his captive. 'Why did you kill him, *señor*?'

'How many times have I told you?' Grimm said. 'I didn't.'

In one flowing movement the officer left the desk and cracked Grimm across the face with his gloved fist. The blow fetched more blood, this time from his nose. Grimm could feel it trickling from his nostril. He was losing count of how many times the bozo had slammed him.

'You were discovered standing over a dead body and you persist in telling me that you didn't even know it was there?' The speaker was of slight build with sloping shoulders. But he could pack a punch; and his dark eyes, piercing from under shaggy eyebrows, showed he enjoyed it. 'You gringos think that Mexicans are stupid. OK, as long as you stay in your own Godless country you can think what you like. But you cross the Rio Grande with your haughty ways, that is another matter.'

Grimm had been hauled roughly down into the basement of the Bureau building, dragged past darkened cells and tied to a chair in an interrogation room. Unventilated, the place reeked of burning kerosene; and other smells, far less pleasant.

The officer strutted round the room threateningly punching an open palm. 'Where are you accommodated?'

Grimm explained the location of his lodgings.

'And what is your business in Mexico?'

Grimm angled his head, his eyes travelling across the peeling plaster of the ceiling. 'I have brought a couple of stud horses that I am aiming to trade.' It was the first thing he thought of.

'And how does murder fit in with horse trading?'

'It doesn't.'

Grimm's head whupped to one side as the fist hit his cheekbone again. 'You are trying my patience. Let me warn you, *señor*, we can do more than just slap you around to get you to talk. Believe me, this is just the beginning.'

Suddenly the door opened and another policeman entered. Low, unintelligible words were exchanged, then the two officers left, closing the door.

Alone, Grimm allowed his head to dangle loosely on his chest. He didn't know how long he could last out. There was a dead man on a slab somewhere and these bozos wanted a conviction; and Black Eyes had decided who it was to be. As these thoughts mulled around his brain he was aware of each beat of his heart resounding through his skull.

He didn't know exactly how long he remained in that unmoving posture. Twenty minutes? Half an hour? He just knew that when the door crashed open again it was too soon. He steeled himself as two officers moved heavily towards him. What next? But this time there were no blows. He was hoisted bodily to his feet so that his bound hands cleared the chair back and he was frog-marched out of the room.

Past the cells, up stone steps, along a corridor. into another room and then dumped unceremoniously on to another chair.

Yet another officer sat opposite him, burly with a balding head that he wiped with a handkerchief. On the desk between them Grimm recognized his own saddle-bags, and their contents strewn over the surface.

'The name is Salinas,' the man went on. 'Captain Salinas. I'm told your name is Jonathan Grimm.'

'That's me.' His jaw hurt as he spoke.

'You must forgive my subordinate,' the chief went on. 'He is somewhat zealous.'

Grimm glanced at Black Eyes, who was now leaning against the wall behind his chief. The prisoner could think of many adjectives to describe the critter who had been exercising his gloved fist on him, but somehow 'zealous' didn't figure amongst them.

'However to give him his due, he has not acted without cause. You are the prime suspect in a murder and you have told him lies. You tell us you are bringing stud horses from the US. We have looked at your horses, *señor*. They are nags. Serviceable, but still nags. In Mexico we pride ourselves on our horse stock. They are not stud horses.'

Grimm shrugged.

The man pointed to the saddle-bags. 'These are yours?'

'Yeah.'

The man nodded and gathered up scattered reward posters. He sheaved through the crumpled documents. 'Why would a horse trader carry such items? And your guns – lovingly maintained – they are fighting weapons. The kind only carried by a man who knows how to use them. Tell me, what are you really doing in Mexico?'

When he had first been dragged to headquarters Grimm had wondered how much he should disclose. Figuring that to admit to his mission wouldn't sit well with being found standing over a dead body he had spun a tale. Seems like now was the time to come clean.

'There is a man called Johnson. He has a price on his head over the border. I am here in search of him.'

'Ah, so now we have another story.' He looked his prisoner up and down. 'Are you now telling us that you are what is called a bounty hunter?'

'That's about the shape of it.'

'Huh, ain't got much dinero in your pockets for a gringo bounty hunter.' The challenge was snarled at him by Black Eyes from his position against the wall.

'We all have our off days,' Grimm grunted. 'The money from my last job fell through. And haven't been paid for the one before that either. Don't get a guaranteed paypacket every Friday in my line. That's the reason I'm down here – looking to earn some folding stuff on another renegade.'

The chief nodded and picked up one of Grimm's Army .44s. 'I see. That would explain this well-used weapon; and your fancy gunbelt.'

He threw a glance at his subordinate. 'You see, Damio. As I told you. There is more to this gringo than meets the eye.'

So the name of the bastard who had been trying to knock his teeth down his throat was Damio. Grimm would remember his name.

The captain stopped nodding and laid the gun back on the desk. 'You know it would be illegal to take someone against their will out of our country?'

'The idea was if I located him I'd find a way to persuade him to accompany me over the Rio Grande. Voluntary like.'

'You seem sure of yourself, *señor*.'

'It was you who concluded that I am not inexperienced in the trade.'

'But, if you are after a big fish, why did you kill a minnow?'

'I didn't.'

'*Mientes, gringo*.' It was Black Eyes again.

The chief raised a hand indicating that the subordinate back off. '*Si*, the *hombre* has lied.'

Grimm felt like he was sinking into quicksand. Funny the things a guy thought of at the darnedest times. Here he was, maybe another beating imminent and he suddenly remembered some fable from schooldays, something about crying wolf but details escaped him. What he did know was: with lying there was always the possibility that being caught out in one thing would give foundation to disbelieve anything else a feller said.

The chief wiped his face once more. 'But whether he is continuing to lie has yet to be seen. Maybe he is learning.' He looked back at the prisoner. 'Anybody vouch for you and the things that you say?'

'Not here in Juarez. Don't know anybody.'

'In the States?'

'As a bounty hunter?'

'Whatever you like. I would be interested in anybody with credibility who'd support your claim to being who you are. You understand, we are in a business where we have learned not to simply accept what an *hombre* chooses to say about himself.'

'If you're willing to send out a wire, there shouldn't be a problem. Law officers in the States have to account for the public money that they pay out to guys like me. They make a record when I do business with them. Legal authorities there will have me on their files.'

'If I wanted to check where should I start?'

'The law office in Constitution. That was the last place I had dealings. Took in an outlaw, name of Louis Burdick. They're on the telegraph. If you ain't happy with a penny ante town like Constitution you could check me out at Fort Smith, Arkansas. I've taken in some desperadoes on Judge Parker's list.'

'Judge Parker, eh? The famous Hanging Judge? Yes, I have heard of him. Well, we shall see.' The chief flicked a hand at his subordinate. 'Now take him to a cell.'

He was manhandled down steps into the depths of the building. It was dark and musty. Unceremoniously he was flung into a cell and a heavy barred door slammed behind him. In the semi-darkness he could just make out another three inmates. Although he couldn't see them distinctly he figured one thing: none of the trio knew the meaning of the word bath, in English or Spanish.

'What you in for?' one growled, after the key had turned and the clip-clop of the warder's boots had faded along the warren.

'Somebody's trying to pin a murder on me.'

'Well, what do you know?' the spokesman grunted, looking at his companions. His eyes adjusting, Grimm discerned smiles on their faces.

'We're four of a kind, *señor*,' the man went on.

Grimm nodded in receipt of the information. Three murderers, he thought, this has got the makings of an interesting night. He wasn't far wrong. The three rose from their pallets and shuffled menacingly towards him. There were times for action but this wasn't one of them. Nor would there be any point in calling for a warder. Grimm had been around enough to know the jailer would probably appreciate being called so he could stand back and watch the fun.

Suddenly two of them shot forward and pinned him roughly against the bars.

'What you got for us, *señor*?' the remaining one asked, his face up close, rancid breath filling the newcomer's nostrils. Grimm didn't speak as the man ripped through his pockets.

Most of his belongings had already been taken so he had nothing but his pipe and tobacco and a few seconds later he didn't have those. When the searcher had satisfied himself that the smoking equipment was the total haul from their new cellmate he displayed his finds to his comrades and invited them to join him.

Freed, Grimm dropped on to a pallet and propped his back against a wall to watch as his tobacco was packed into the pipe. A match flared, smoke inhaled, and the instrument was passed around the cell.

When Grimm was allowed a turn in the ritual he concluded, or at least hoped, that he had now paid the price for an undisturbed night.

TEN

It was well into the next morning and Grimm was back in the police chief's office. He'd had an uncomfortable night on a hard pallet but had not been further disturbed by the other occupants.

'I'm trusting my own judgement here,' the chief said. He had some telegraph messages on the desk before him. 'I think you are who you say you are. Your appearance fits the description that's come in over the wire this morning.'

The bounty hunter was tall, gaunt of feature with a scatter of black powder burnt into his cheek, a relic from his war days. Like many of the men he usually sought: pretty easy to describe.

'You got no obvious motive for the killing last night and a search of the area didn't reveal the murder weapon.' He went to the window and looked at a gaggle of street urchins in the plaza. 'The blood was well dried. Looks like he died quite a bit earlier than when my men found you with the body. And the money in his wallet untouched. Nothing conclusive but taking one thing with another, I don't think you did it.'

'When did you come to that conclusion?'

'Last night, I guess.'

'And you still locked me away?'

The man grunted. 'I was still in need of some confirmation on your identity and I couldn't use the telegraph till this morning. What is more, I figured you'd needed a lesson that you can't come down here ignoring our laws.' He turned and pointed to Grimm's gunbelt and belongings on the table. 'So now you are free to go, *señor.*'

Grimm ran his fingers lightly over his tender face. 'You got a place where I can clean up?'

The chief indicated a door at the side of his office. Without a word, Grimm crossed the room and entered. There was a pitcher, bowl and other washing accoutrements. A bloodied face looked back at him through the cracked mirror.

Minutes later he returned and picked up his things. The officer watched him as he checked the loads in his gun, and said, 'I do not want any trouble, *Señor* Grimm. I know from the wire that you have killed many men. At this stage I am not deporting you. But if you identify this *hombre* that you seek – this Francisco Johnson – you do not take any independent action. You inform me. Is that understood?'

'Understood.'

'But, if you'll take some advice from me, you'll head back over the Rio Grande right now. I have not heard of the *hombre* whom you seek. You are a stranger in a strange country. Your task will be next to impossible.'

'Yeah, I know I've come down here on a long

shot but, now I'm here, you any objection to me staying over a mite longer and doing some enquiring?'

Salinas considered the matter while he watched the man pick up his gunbelt. 'Like I said, I'm not deporting you so you are free to ask your questions. But there is to be no more trouble – and you keep me informed of anything you unearth.'

'Agreed,' Grimm said, swinging the belt around his hips. 'One thing's bugging me,' he added as he fixed the buckle. 'Last night, how come your boys were so fast on the scene? I stumble accidentally on to a dead man; next minute uniforms are all over the place.'

'Information received.'

'If that was the case hasn't it occurred to you this could have been a set-up? Somebody trying to frame me? Have you checked out who gave you the information?'

'It was a scribbled note. No one recalls seeing who delivered it.'

'Seems to me, there's your killer.'

'Maybe.'

The chief returned to his desk and glanced at one of the wires. 'It says here,' he announced, as Grimm had his hand of the door handle, 'that they call you the Reaper.'

Grim was irritated by the label. 'Not really. Something a hick journalist put in a paper once.'

'Seems to have stuck, *señor*.'

'Colourful fancy sells more papers than reality. The newsboys down here must operate the same way. You know what they say: if there's a choice between fact and legend, print the legend.'

'Still, you carry a rep for killing the men you seek. Seems to me that's somewhat inefficient.'

'Or efficient, depending on how you look at it.'

The chief nodded. '*Adios*. I trust I will not be seeing you again in this office.'

Grimm walked through the door. 'I hope I don't find they sold my horses and gear when I get back to the rooming-house. The way this country operates it's an even bet.'

The chief waited until he'd gone, then said to his assistant, 'I still want to know what that *hombre*'s up to.' He looked again out of the window at the urchins. 'Get one of those *muchachos* to keep an eye on him. They'll do anything for a handful of pesos.'

* * *

From the other side of the plaza Grimm watched the worshippers coming to the Mission. Eventually he was rewarded by seeing the Libertad buggy bearing the Señorita Consuela. The vehicle pulled in near the steps. The driver helped the *señorita* down, then returned to the driving seat while the woman went into the church.

Grimm crossed the plaza and leant against an adobe wall. Eventually the service was over and the crowds began spilling down the steps. As the *señorita* emerged he stepped alongside her. 'Excuse me, *señorita*. With your permission, I'd like a word.'

She quickened her pace. 'You again. I have nothing to say.'

From his position near the buggy, the driver had been watching. 'Everything all right, Señorita Consuela?' he asked when they reached him.

'Take me home,' she said.

'Hold on there a moment,' Grimm said. 'All I want is a short talk.'

'You heard the *señorita*,' the driver snapped. But before he knew what was happening Grimm had yanked his arm up his back and spun him round. He pulled the man's gun from its holster and gently but firmly levered the Mexican's backside with his foot so that he was propelled forward. 'Take a walk, *muchacho*. I'm only gonna be couple of minutes.'

Consuela nodded towards the man. 'Do as he says, Eduardo. We don't want to make a spectacle in the middle of town.'

The disarmed man stepped away a few more paces and stood scowling at the Anglo. Grimm helped the woman into the buggy and sat beside her, keeping his eye on Eduardo.

'What's happened to your face?' she asked coldly.

He ignored her question. 'Listen, I wanna know what's going on.'

'I don't know what you're talking about.'

'Where have I heard that before? Don't mess with me, lady. Somebody killed Carlos Medillo and tried to pin it on me. Who and why?'

'I still don't know what you're talking about.'

'It's got something to do with Winchy Johnson, ain't it?' He caught some reaction in her eyes. 'Francisco Johnson,' he went on. 'Yeah, it's something to do with him, ain't it?'

She forced composure back into her eyes and remained silent.

'What do you know about him?' Grimm went on.

Still silence.

'Where is he?'

Suddenly capitulation showed in her face. 'You want to know where he is, Mr Big Americano?' Her voice was cracking. 'He's thirty miles from here. That's where he is.'

'Where?'

'Chilata.'

'Now we're getting somewhere, lady. Where-abouts exactly?'

'Exactly? Chilata Cemetery. That's where exactly.'

Grimm let it sink in. 'Tell me more.'

'We were lovers. We were going to get married. My brother was against it because Francisco was a *bandido*. Anyway, Ruiz's opposition was academic. The *federales* caught up with Francisco. There was a gun battle. He was killed.' She sobbed a little. 'We buried him in Chilata Cemetery.'

'When was this?'

'Three years ago this fall.'

'And what about this Carlos Medillo?'

'I know nothing of his death.'

Grimm figured he'd got as much as he was

going to get out of the woman. He nodded. 'Sorry to put you through this, *señorita*.' He beckoned to the watching driver and placed the man's gun on the seat. He stepped down and touched his hat to the woman. Still scowling the driver pulled himself up into the buggy and settled himself into the driving position.

Grimm stepped back and watched it roll away.

ELEVEN

In the shade of a juniper Grimm stood on a hill looking down at the cemetery of Chilata. It was a sun-drenched midday and he was sticky and tired after his long ride. Half-way down the slope a burial service was being conducted. The slight breeze carried faint snatches of the padre's words.

Grimm tied his horse to the tree and began to scrutinize the grave markers one by one. Death was said to be the great leveller but even in their big sleep people were distinguished on a social basis. Some names were crudely etched on weathering wooden stumps while others were grandly carved in stone, assorted Virgin Marys, cherubim and angels to watch over them.

The mourners were making their sad way back up the slope when he found the one he was looking for. A modest stone slab bearing the name Francisco Johnson. It had to be the one. There couldn't be many Francisco Johnsons in Chilata. There couldn't be many Francisco Johnsons in the whole of Mexico. He looked down at it and read the dates that summarized the span of life.

Had he travelled nearly 200 miles for this? Was this *adios*, three grand? Yet another pay-day vaporizing before his eyes?

He took off his hat and wiped his brow, looked across the dormitory of death beds, silent now save for the buzz of insects. The mourners were disappearing over the top of the hill, leaving a solitary gravedigger to complete the final filling-in.

Grimm heavy-footed down to the toiling Mexican. '*Buenos dias, señor.*'

The man looked up, returned the greeting then resumed his task.

'You mind if I sit here awhiles?' Grimm asked. 'Been in the saddle since sun-up.'

The man glanced up. 'I do not mind, *señor*. And I don't think you will get many complaints from those taking their last rest here.'

As the man returned to his labour, Grimm instinctively felt for his pipe and cursed to himself when he remembered its fate. Aloud he said, 'You been the gravedigger here at Chilata very long?'

'Man and boy, *señor*. And my father before me. May Our Virgin bless him.' He paused to look heavenward and sign himself. 'It is good that a man has a place. I have a place: gravedigger to the good people of Chilata. I know my job and can handle it. Mind, it is thirsty work, *señor*.'

Grimm nodded up the hill. 'I have a water canteen with my horse. You're welcome to share it.'

The man laughed. 'Water? Ah. This ancient overworked body needs more than water.' He put down his shovel and walked across to a blanket bag. He thrust his hand inside and came up with a towelled bundle that he unwrapped to reveal a tequila bottle. 'Now you, *amigo*, are welcome to share this with me.' He uncorked it and passed it across.

Grimm took a swig and wiped the rim before passing it back. '*Gracias.*'

The gravedigger took a long draught and smacked his lips. 'It is not only thirsty work but lonely too. The only one I have for conversation up here is the padre. But he is a sombre fellow. There are my friends.' He waved at the markers. 'They are good listeners. But that is all.' He laughed, took another swig and passed the bottle again to his companion.

They continued that way as the sun journeyed across the clear sky, and the bottle journeyed to and fro between them. After a time they could have been life-long *amigos* in a cantina.

'Came to see an *amigo* of mine,' Grimm said. It was his turn with the bottle and he waved it towards the grave that he had identified. 'Francisco Johnson. You know the name?'

'I know the names of all my slumbering flock, *señor*. Their names are etched in my brain as well as on the stone and wood. Francisco Johnson. Put the dirt over him, some two, three years ago.'

'Well, I was passing through and thought I'd come and pay my last respects.'

The man stiffened. 'You in the same business, *señor*?'

'Naw. We were young together. We parted

trails long ways before he turned *bandido*.'

'That is good, *señor*. I trust you won't mind me speaking plain about your friend, but he was very bad *bandido*. Thief, killed anybody who got in his way. They say he loved killing so much his speciality was killing for payment.'

He got up and went to his bag. 'I got food here, *señor*. It is lunchtime. You will break bread with me?'

'If it ain't too much trouble.'

'It is no trouble, *señor*. I have enough. My woman, she always gives me too much.' He patted his fat gut. 'This damn thing gets in the way of my digging these days.'

They worked their way through a mountain of bread and cheese. Grimm welcomed the change from the goat meat that had been his fare whilst in the country.

'I have enjoyed your company, *señor*,' the gravedigger said as he finished off the bottle. The words came a little slurred. 'Not many folk stop to talk to a gravedigger.'

He dropped the empty bottle into the bag and when it clinked against glass he chuckled and, in an ungainly fashion, put his finger against his lips. 'Shh, do not tell the padre, *señor*. As you might have gathered from that noise, that ain't the first I had today.' He became serious and looked at Grimm with eyes that took some time to focus. 'How close were you and your friend?'

'Well, when we were young, mighty close. But ain't seen him for – what is it? – must be twenty years.'

The man's fingers went to his lips again as one does when imparting secrets. 'Do not feel too sad for your *amigo*. I ain't told anybody this before. But you, being a close friend....'

'Yes?'

'Do not mourn too much for him, *señor*. For I do not think he is dead.'

'What makes you say a thing like that?'

'He was a much wanted *bandido*. The *federales* were after him and they cornered him in a barn. A hacienda not too far from Chilata. There was a shoot-out. But he wouldn't give up. Then they tried to burn him out. But he still wouldn't come out. He never came out. He burned to death.'

'So?'

'That was the way it appeared. But, you know, many *federales* are former *bandidos*. They work hand in hand. It is my reckoning that some of his old *compadres* in uniform worked his escape.'

'But you buried him.'

'I buried somebody. It is not widely known but there were two outlaws. The soldiers only fetched out one body. So badly burned you couldn't tell who it was. I know because I saw what was left in the box. It was claimed to be Johnson's and that was it. No sane man questions the *federales*, *señor*. In Mexico they are next to God himself.'

'Are you sure about him?'

'I am not sure, *señor*. But there has always been a whisper.'

So that was it. Johnson had covered his tracks and was still alive and kicking. The bounty was still up for grabs. The Reaper was back in business. What was more, his dodger on Johnson was an old one. There was an even chance the ante was now higher than three grand.

* * *

Back in Juarez Captain Salinas had been thinking about the man named Grimm. Had he told the truth about his reasons for being in Juarez? For sure the man was no knucklehead fresh off the boat. He knew from the communications he had received that, if this was the same Jonathan Grimm, the *hombre* was known Stateside to be skilled with his weapons, a man who operated in the shadows. As long as such a man was in Juarez the police chief wanted to know his where-at. *Caramba*, he had enough on his plate without a loose cannon sliding all over the decks. So he had been glad when the urchin tailing him had reported back that Grimm had ridden south. He would like to know what the Americano was up to, where he was going, but he couldn't afford to have a man following the bounty hunter all over Mexico. He hoped he was permanently out of his hair.

There was a knock at the door and Damio came in, placing a piece of paper on the chief's desk. 'The Justice Department have just set the date for the trial. Next Monday.'

Salinas studied the paper.

TWELVE

Out of Chilata Grimm headed north-east. The geography in his head told him it would not be too much of a detour to take in the Libertad during his return journey and, as he was still inquisitive about the place, he didn't want to miss an opportunity. It was fairly open country and he only had to ask his way once.

Come evening he was once again on the periphery of the Libertad spread. He left his horse in a brush thicket and, keeping to the shadows of shrubs and trees, worked his way down to the hacienda on foot. Here and there he could make out a figure. It was clear they were sentries but, expecting nobody, they were not exceptionally vigilant, and were easily bypassed. Nearer the buildings he recognized the layout from his first visit so that the increasing darkness did not pose a problem and he easily identified the hacienda from the clutch of buildings that made up the complex. Eventually he was crouched beside the adobe wall of a corral beyond which he could hear horses and mules eating hay.

He inched his way along the wall until he reached the end. There was open space between his position and the main building. He waited for cloud to obscure the moon; then loped across the gap. Flattened against the casa wall he waited to check that he was still unnoticed, then slowly worked his way around it until he saw light marking a window. He could hear voices emanating from it.

He got as close as he could, adjacent to the aperture, and remained stock still, proned against the cool flatness of the wall. There were two. One voice he pegged as belonging to Don Ruiz, the other he didn't recognize. For a long time there was nothing significant in the exchange until he thought he heard someone use a word that sounded like 'Johnson'. For some moments he wasn't sure, his command of Spanish being rudimentary, then the unfamiliar one said, 'I have told you, *señor*, it makes me uneasy having Johnson about.'

'Don't fret, Lopez,' Don Ruiz said. 'It won't be for long.'

'But why did it have to be him, *señor*?'

'You know he is the best man.'

In terms of use to the eavesdropper that seemed to be it as the conversation trailed off in another direction. But what he had heard was enough for the present. His detour to the Libertad had not been in vain. The possibility of which he had learned at Chilata had firmed up: Johnson was alive. And up to some deviltry by the sound of it. But what? And what did 'having

Johnson about' mean? Was Johnson here at the Libertad itself? Or in Juarez? Or somewhere nearby?

For a long time Grimm stood there but could pick up no more information. Well, one thing was for sure: he couldn't stand there till the light of morning exposed him. Stealthily he moved away from the buildings and began to work his way up the grade.

His horse was glad to sense his rider and began a whinny that Grimm just managed to stifle by stroking the animal's muzzle. However, his attempt at quieting the animal was of no benefit. In his absence a sentry had already discovered the tethered horse and was waiting behind the tree. The Mexican chose this moment to step forward. Grimm heard the movement and turned so that he caught the descending pistol butt on the side of the head instead of the back. But he still dropped senseless to the ground.

The *caballero* checked the man was out and disarmed him. Then he called a companion and the two of them dragged the intruder down to the hacienda. Grimm was dumped on the pavings at the edge of the courtyard and watched by one while the other went to notify Don Ruiz.

The *ranchero* came, the *caballero* leading the way with an oil-lamp. The Don looked down at the still unconscious man. 'It's that nosy gringo again,' he said when he had examined the face illuminated by the lamp.

'*Si, señor*,' one hand said. 'The one we tried to pin Carlos's murder on.'

'Thought we'd killed two birds with one stone with that job,' the Don said, 'but we didn't do enough fixing for the charge to stick. I wonder what his game is.'

'There is a rumour in Juarez, *señor*, that he is a bounty hunter.'

'If that's the case, he could be after Johnson.' The Don pondered a little more. 'No matter. By delivering himself to us on a plate he has solved whatever difficulty he could have presented to us.' He looked up the slope into the darkness. 'Kill him and dump his body somewhere. Doesn't matter where as long as he's a good deal off Libertad land.'

'No problem, *señor*.'

At that point Grimm began to stir.

'Hit him again,' Ruiz said. 'Hard, a couple of times to make sure.'

One of the *caballeros* pulled his gun and was about to administer the blows when a voice came from the hacienda.

'What's going on out there?'

It was the Don's sister.

'Nothing for you to worry your pretty head about, Consuela,' the Don said aloud, adding in a whisper, 'Drag the *hombre* out of sight. *Riba, riba.*'

The woman stepped on to the veranda and peered into the darkness that marked the edge of the courtyard. She could just make out a form on the ground. 'Is one of the men sick?'

Don Ruiz could hear shoes clip-clopping over the slabs and turned to see his sister approaching fast. 'Put that thing away,' he hissed to the *caballero* with the poised gun.

'Why, that's the Americano who came looking for work the other day,' Consuela said when she could make out Grimm's features. 'What's happened? Has there been an accident?'

'Kind of,' the *ranchero* said, successfully masking his annoyance at being thwarted. 'One of the guards knocked him out in the darkness. Mistook him for a prowler.'

Grimm groaned as consciousness returned along with a sense that a train had hit the side of his head.

'The poor man needs attention,' the woman said. She waved her arms at the two *caballeros*, ordering them to bring him in, and turned to head towards the hacienda.

The *vaqueros* looked at their boss for guidance and he shrugged to indicate that they should comply with the *rancho* mistress's orders. Still groggy, Grimm was helped through the building and into the kitchen. A couple of servants were preparing a meal and they paused in their task. A chair was found for the injured man and the *caballeros* were dismissed. Consuela took a bowl of water and began bathing his wound.

'There is only a graze, *señor*,' she said after an appraisal, 'but there will be a nasty bruise and swelling by morning.'

'It was my own fault,' Grimm said.

'How come you ran into one of our guards?'

'Ran into one of your guards?' he chuckled without mirth. 'More like he ran into me.' He returned to giving some kind of answer to her question. 'Lost my bearings. Shouldn't have been on Libertad land at all.'

The *señorita* continued the tending in silence. When she had completed the task she passed the bowl and cloths to one of the servants.

As the objects were taken away she surveyed her handiwork. 'If you are well enough to eat you are welcome to dine with us this evening. That is the least we can do after inflicting such an injury on an innocent traveller.'

There was no denying he was hungry. He'd had nothing since the graveside cheese and bread at noon. 'That would pleasure me, ma'am.'

* * *

There were only the three of them at the candle-lit table. Despite the Don's polite conversation, Grimm was aware of an underlying hostility. There was a side to the man and his affairs that he kept from his sister. That was plain.

After a while Consuela looked across the table at her brother. 'On his first visit here *Señor* Grimm was in search of work and you told him there was none to be had. Could you not now offer him employment, as a gesture of regret for the unfortunate mistake that has resulted in injury to him?'

For a second Grimm glimpsed the other side of the *ranchero* in his eyes. A hard annoyance flickered for a moment. The man was big and powerful but sought to avoid conflict with his sister. He thought on the suggestion for a few seconds. 'I suppose he could be found a position, in the circumstances. *Si*, we could use extra labour for the round-up. It is not for a few weeks but *Señor* Grimm could use the time to familiarize himself with the outfit and get to know the rest of the boys.'

The man wanted Grimm dead. Regaining some consciousness on the outskirts of the courtyard, Grimm had heard vague words around him. In his semi-aware state they hadn't made much sense. Not then. But his alert brain had cast back, rejigged the memories to give them meaning. From what he recalled now, sounded like the Don had told his men to kill Grimm and dump the body. If that was his aim, having the man on the *rancho* would make the task easier. If Grimm stayed here surrounded by Don Ruiz's Mexican lackeys his life wouldn't be worth a plumb peso.

'No, thank you, sir,' he said. 'I've had a change of plans since we last spoke together. I'll be heading back to the States soon.'

'Well, the offer's there,' the Don said.

'What are your plans for tonight?' Consuela asked. 'I hope they don't include riding back to Juarez. I must tell you, you look very pale, *señor*.'

Grimm had wondered if it showed. He still felt a mite light-headed and had only managed to pick at his food. 'You're right, ma'am. Ain't quite got my sea-legs back.'

'That fixes it. It would not be wise to attempt the return journey tonight. You are staying here.' She called a name and a servant scurried in to whom she gave instructions for the airing and preparation of a guest room.

'I think you're right, ma'am,' Grimm said. 'That's very kind.'

'I attend mass at the Guadalupe Mission in the morning. If you are well you can ride into town with me in the buggy. Your horse can follow on.'

THIRTEEN

The buggy drew up outside the Guadelupe Mission in Juarez. Grimm was not only thankful for the ride into town, he was thankful for being able to get off the Libertad property with breath in his body. If it hadn't have been for the innocent intervention of the woman he figured he wouldn't have seen daybreak.

Before debouching, he leaned towards Consuela and spoke in a whisper such that the driver couldn't hear. '*Señorita*, I appreciate your hospitality last night – the meal and a pillow on which to rest this aching head of mine – but I'm gonna have to start talking turkey for a spell. Fact is, I got a question.' He paused, watching her eyes before he asked, 'Why are you so anxious for me to think that Francisco Johnson is dead?'

'Anxious, *señor*? I do not understand.'

He could tell by the sudden change in her face that she did understand something so he remained silent to encourage her to continue.

'He is dead,' she went on, 'and that is that.'

'When one of your brother's men nearly

108

brained me last night I was on the way back from Chilata. You remember Chilata?'

'Of course I know it. It is a place of sadness for me.'

The introduction of emotion was a sidetrack for Grimm. 'It's where you said Johnson is buried. Well, *señorita*, there are those in that village who believe that Johnson did not die and that it is not his body in the grave.'

'That cannot be so.'

He maintained his scrutiny of her eyes. Did she mean it? Hard to tell. 'I'm just telling you what I know, lady.'

One thing he could tell: there was to be nothing else forthcoming from her. Deciding to discontinue his probing he dropped down and freed the reins of his horse.

'*Adios, Señorita,*' he said, touching his hat, and began to lead his horse across the plaza in the direction of the road that led to his lodgings. Eventually he was making his way over recognized sun-hardened ruts, not noticing that he had been spotted by a *rurale* seated outside a cantina. Nor did he see the *rurale* get up and head for the Police Bureau after he had passed.

What he did know was that after he had quartered his horse and was coming out of the stable, he came face to face with a couple of sweat-stained uniforms. 'The chief would like to see you, *señor*,' one said. Grimm nodded and allowed himself to be escorted to the now familiar public building.

'Your injuries have been added to, *señor*,' the

chief said when Grimm was standing before his desk. 'That's a nasty looking bump you got there.'

'Fell off my horse.'

'You still poking your nose where it is not wanted?'

'Like I said, fell off my horse.'

'Have it your way. Point is, last time we met I told you I wanted you heading north over the Rio Grande, yet the next thing I know you're riding south.'

'The way I remember it, it was advice, not an order.'

'And now you are back in town.'

The man was doing no more than proving that he had eyes. 'Yeah, I'm back in town. I know you've had your share of political troubles here in Mexico but it's still something of a free country as far as I heard.'

'Where did you go?'

'Chilata.'

'What for?'

'Did some enquiring. You know, about that hombre Johnson I was telling you about. Heard tell he was dead and buried out there.'

'And you confirmed that he is.' Salinas's tone suggested a statement rather than a question.

'I thought you hadn't heard of him.'

'I hadn't. I am not a man of this region. I was transferred from San Cristobal not too long back. Anyway, after our first meeting I made some enquiries. It has been difficult because systematic record-making is not a strong point of the Chihuahua force. But I eventually found that he was known to us. And that he had been tracked by the *federales* and killed in the subsequent confrontation at Chilata. So, *amigo*, that is the end of your search. And of your reason for being in Mexico.'

'Not quite.'

'Why not?'

'Figure there's a strong possibility he didn't die like you and everyone else seems to think.'

'And what leads you to that supposition?'

'Something an old man said.' He described his exchange with the gravedigger.

'Sounds like the ramblings of an old mescal drinker. You know, such a job is boring. Some oldsters like to romanticize. Makes their task of digging holes a little more interesting.'

'Mebbe.'

'I do not want your unfounded doubts to provide an excuse for staying here. You are a man of trouble and it is still my feeling that the sooner you are back north of the border the better. Is that understood?'

Grimm nodded.

The police chief readjusted his sitting position. 'When you were seen entering town again you were in the company of Señorita Galinas de Zedari.'

'Yeah.'

'The Libertad spread is not on the way back to Juarez.'

'I'm still a stranger in these parts. Got lost on my way back from Chilata and wandered on to their property.'

'That where you fell off your horse?'

'Yes. They were good enough to feed me and give me a bed for the night.'

'You know Don Ruiz?'

'I've met him a couple of times.'

'Could be bad for you to associate with him, *señor*.'

Grimm waited and then flicked a hand to and fro. 'This flow of information you have talked about – it work both ways?'

'I don't understand, *señor*.'

'You of a mind to explain what you just said about Don Ruiz? Seems like a square guy, well set up in the local community.'

The chief thought about it. 'Don't see as it'd do any harm to tell you a few things.' The tone of his voice had changed. 'I don't know why but I think can trust you. *Caramba*, a man needs to trust somebody. Well, my friend, the Don is not what he seems. He has one of the biggest spreads in the region and a herd to match it. But there were many deaths in the building up of his land. Anybody who stood in the way of his expanding his property got despatched to meet his Maker. All mysterious deaths that the Department couldn't get evidence on.'

'This doesn't come as a surprise. I have to confess to misleading you earlier on. I didn't fall off my horse.' He touched the lump on his head. 'This was his boys' doing. He was gonna have me killed out there. If his sister hadn't happened upon the scene he would have seen it through.'

'Ha.' The chief absorbed the news, then said,

'Have you seen or heard something you shouldn't?'

'Not that I know of.'

'Interesting. You see, on top of the past killings there's every sign he's at the centre of cattle rustling across the whole of the Chihuahua region.'

'If you know these things why isn't he behind bars by now?'

'He is a *caudillo*.'

'*Caudillo*?'

The chief slid open a drawer and pulled out a bottle. 'Hey, *señor*, you take a drink with a greaseball?' His tone had completely changed.

Grimm chuckled. 'Be an honour.'

'Then pull up a chair,' the man said and a couple of glasses suddenly appeared magically in his hand.

'If you are to survive in this country, Señor Grimm,' he went on when they had wet their throats, 'there are things you should know. Mexico, she is not only different from your United States, she is different from all the other countries in South America. In Mexico a small number of people, the *caudillos*, they own everything; most of the population own nothing. Unlike your country, or any country of which I have heard, there is no in between. No middle classes. Can you imagine that? Is it any wonder our peoples have been at each others' throats for centuries?'

He went to the window. 'The land out there. Is no good. Cannot grow much. Nowhere in

Mexico. We had good land once: Arizona, California, New Mexico, Texas. But you Americanos took it from us. Now the people are lucky to get food in their bellies. So, if you are lucky enough to get a job as a policeman or a government position, you don't do it for any grand principles. You have no high-falutin' ideas of being a public servant. You do it so you have power and can dip your bread in some gravy.'

He looked back at Grimm. 'Many policemen were bandits before they put on uniform. They lick the asses of the *caudillos* and squeeze the blood out of everybody else. I can't trust those below me. And I can't trust those above me. I just do my job and watch my back.'

He paused. 'I'm not an angel. I take a free meal now and then. But I don't take regular kick-backs. Nor protection money. No officer tortures the shit out of somebody just to get their own way, not while I'm around. You see, I am one of the few who have some principles. Oh, not because I am a goody-goody. I'm not trying to sell you that idea. But if somebody doesn't try to do what is right our country will stay in the gutter for ever.'

He chuckled. 'I can see it in your eyes. Who's to say that I'm not like the rest? you are asking yourself. All I can say is that if I was, I wouldn't be talking to you like this.'

He noted Grimm's empty glass and topped it up. 'As I was saying about Don Ruiz. He is a big wheel in stolen beef. I have given up trying to get evidence. His men always seem to know when we've set up an operation.'

'Informers in uniform?'

'*Si*. They can be at all levels.' He lowered his voice. 'My own transfer here was to replace a head of police who was suspected of being, shall we say, too much in the shade.' He shook his finger at the floor. 'When you were our guest in the cells below, did you see three prisoners there?'

'Yeah. I had the honour of their company.'

'Well, they constitute my ace in the hole. They were sighted out in *baranca* country with a stolen herd heading for the Libertad. There was a shoot-out. They killed a couple of my men and got away. Anyway, we picked them up later. They won't admit anything. Won't confess to the killings. And won't admit to working for the Don. They're sitting quiet, and confident that the trial will be mere routine and they'll soon be walking free again.'

Grimm nodded. 'They didn't strike me as men in fear of their lives.'

'They have no fear of the court. They are gunslinging *peons* with no more than a handful of pesos to their names yet they have an expensive lawyer.'

'Financed by Don Ruiz?'

The chief chuckled sardonically. 'More than likely but there's so many middle men in between that a direct connection couldn't be proved. But they have me to deal with now. I am not one who bends in the wind. And what they don't know is I've got a witness. Name of Sanchez. He's a reliable witness and it's pretty certain they'll get convicted and face the firing squad. When they realize there is nothing else the Don can do for them, then it's on the cards that they'll start talking in the hopes of striking some kind of a deal. If they do squeal, that'll be the end of the Don. I'll get him on rustling and being complicit in murder. And I'll have their confession to back it up.'

'If he is a *caudillo* as powerful as you say, and there are informers on your staff, won't he know you have a witness?'

'Maybe. But I've got the guy hidden away. I won't bring him into view until the trial.'

'Mebbe they already know where he is.'

The man shook his head. 'There's only me and two trusted officers who know his whereabouts.'

FOURTEEN

The police bureau behind him, Grimm squared his hat on his head and set off across the plaza.

'*Buenos dias, señor.*'

Turning to see the diminutive Ricardo walking in step with him, Grimm returned the greeting.

'The gringo has been visiting once again with the police.'

Grimm chuckled. 'You sure got big eyes, *muchacho*. Is there anything happens in Juarez you don't know about?'

'And did I not earlier see the gringo step from the carriage of the Señorita Galinas de Zedari?'

'You did.'

'Does the gringo mind if I give him a word of warning?'

'Go ahead.'

'The *señorita* has a brother, the Don Ruiz. It is advisable for someone such as yourself to keep much distance between himself and Don Ruiz. He is a much bad *hombre*.'

This was the one sure thing Grimm had learned during his Mexican stay but he feigned ignorance. 'Why do you say that?'

'He treats badly those with whom he deals, *señor*.'

'Such as?'

'He forces the poorest *peons* to sell their cotton crops to him. He pays in pesos much below the market price. I know. I have a cousin who suffers from his dealings with the Don.'

'Why don't your cousin sell to some other dealer at the market price?'

'Such an action results in a far higher price. Things happen, senor. Places get burned. *Peons* have accidents in the dark. Sometimes they just disappear.'

Grimm thought on it. 'I thought Don Ruiz was a *ranchero*. Horses and cattle. I didn't know he was in cotton.'

'He has a finger in many pies, *señor*. He is the biggest *caudillo* in these parts.' He pointed vaguely to the east. 'He has a big cotton warehouse on the edge of town. The gringo must have seen it?'

Grimm stopped his horse. 'No. Where exactly?'

When Ricardo had explained, the man thanked him in the usual way. '*Gracias*, kid,' he said as the boy pocketed the coins. 'Be seeing you.'

As he walked alone towards his lodgings he mulled over the new item of information. This Don Ruiz was an even bigger *honcho* than he had thought. And he was at the centre of some bad doings. He didn't know exactly what but he knew that Johnson figured in it somewhere.

What to do next?

Still not having come up with a plan, he followed Ricardo's directions making his way to the cotton warehouse to give it the once-over. It didn't take him long to get there and he found it to be a large building. He stood across the street watching labourers unloading huge bales from wagons. Keeping his distance he sauntered casually around the place, examining it from all sides. By the time he was back at the front the labourers had finished shifting the consignment and were closing the doors.

The more he had learned about the Don the more inquisitive he had become. Maybe a look around the inside of the warehouse would have merit. But it would have to be after dark.

* * *

He waited until the night had closed in then returned to the place on foot, not knowing what he was looking for or what he would find. Behind him the distant lights of Juarez winked but no lights showed from the large building. He gained access at the rear and found himself amongst stacks of cotton bales. In the darkness he stood still for a spell, taking stock. The air was musty; here and there he heard faint creaks; but they were only the groanings of an unoccupied, cavernous wooden building. When his eyes had accustomed to the darkness he worked his way between the hulks of stacked merchandise.

Near the front he could make out an office.

He was getting close when he heard the sound of feet on planking outside. He backtracked as a key rattled in a lock. He was well into the depths of the warehouse and behind a pillar of cotton bales as the front door swung open. For a brief second figures were dimly silhouetted against the grey of the night outside.

Two men entered and the door closed. The shapes clunked through the front recesses of the building, then a light flared in the office as an oil-lamp was lit. He peered cautiously from his hiding place. He could see the men behind the glass. One was the Don.

'Hope he is not long,' the Don said. The voice was muffled.

'He is reliable, *señor*.'

Grimm began to move forward so that he could hear voices more distinctly when again came the sound of boots on wooden boards. He retreated once more to find refuge behind a stack of bales. By the time he was out of sight and peering back, someone had come in and was just entering the office.

'Good to see you, Francisco,' the Don said.

So Francisco Johnson was alive; and here in this very building! Yet he was hidden from view. 'Everything is all set. I have a gun which cannot be traced back.'

'Good. Exactly how are you going to work it?'

'I've scouted out the Mission. It's a good spot. The campanile gives a good vantage of the road to the law court. From what we know that's the direction in which the *rurales* will be bringing the witness. There'll be no trouble getting in a killing shot from there.'

So that was what it was all about. Johnson had been called in to assassinate the witness against the three killers.

'You think you'll have enough time to get away?' the Don asked.

'I've cased the inside – enough to identify the quickest way out. It'll only take seconds to descend the top flight of steps. There's a window at the top of the landing that opens out on to the roof. Then it's across the roof, down at the rear then back to my crib.' He laughed. 'They'll be looking for a professional, not bar-room sweepings like me.'

'You know your business, but it still sounds tight to me.'

'As you say, I know my business. I have some firecrackers. Miguel will be stationed at the far side of the plaza. The moment he hears the shot he puts a match to the firecrackers. As it is, it's difficult to locate a single unexpected shot. The firecrackers going off so close on the shot will add to the confusion. The report from my gun along with the firework explosions will be echoing all round the plaza. A moment's confusion is all I need.'

'What about the padre?'

'No problem. It won't take much to get him out of the way for a short spell.'

'Lopez,' the Don said, 'open up that bottle of mescal. We'll have a drink on it.'

Despite the movement required in sharing the

drinks Grimm still couldn't see the assassin.

There was a long pause, then the stranger said, 'Don't get any ideas about trying to get rid of me.'

The Don chuckled. 'Never entered my head, Francisco.'

'The hell it didn't.'

'*Señor*, you are my sister's man. Family.'

'Nevertheless an accident to me would get you off the hook and seal the whole thing up neat as a gunny-sack. Don't even think about it. I've left a message explaining the whole deal which goes to the police chief should anything happen to me.'

'Now that was not friendly. There was no need, *señor*. You and I go back a long way.'

'Insurance. I know all the tricks. I'm a professional. That's why you are paying me so much.'

There was another pause then Johnson said, 'Well, thanks for the drink. Now all I need is a good night's shuteye.'

Grimm felt irritated. He had come this far but he still didn't know what Johnson looked like. He moved forward to get a closer look as they began making movements to leave but before they came out of the office one of them doused the lamp. Now there would be no way of getting a close look inside. He soft-footed back to the rear door and slipped quietly outside. Hell, there was a Mexican standing watch over the horses preventing him from getting closer. He proned himself in the shadows against the wall as the three men came out. Too dark to identify anybody. Then they were away into the night.

FIFTEEN

How should he play this? What he would have preferred was to take Johnson in tow before tomorrow's caper. Then it would be simply a matter of trussing up the varmint and riding out of town where he could find a quiet place to cross the Rio Grande without being seen.

The hitch with that was he still didn't know what Johnson looked like, or where he was holing up. He knew one thing: the man was going to try an assassination from the top of the Mission campanile tomorrow. He knew the basic details of the plot. One course of action was to stake out the Guadalupe Mission early and stop Johnson before he got in his shot. On the face of it the hunter would get his man. But there were complications. When the police chief arrived on the scene he would want to know what Grimm was doing at the Mission in the first place. It wouldn't wash that he had just stumbled accidentally on an assassination attempt; just in the nick of time too. Even a half-wit would guess that he had to know something beforehand. The captain was no lame-brain; and he had made it plain he wanted to be kept in the picture. The more Grimm got involved in this thing the more certain he became of one thing: he needed the captain's co-operation if he was going to get any dinero out of this Mexican jaunt.

As he walked along the darkened street he thought it over. The final option was to tell the police chief now. It stuck in his craw like a hunk of unchewed goat meat, but by all figuring there seemed no alternative.

There were a few dim lights coming from the Bureau windows when he arrived out front.

'Like to see Captain Salinas,' he told the desk officer.

'The capitan is not here, *señor*,' the uniformed man on the desk said. 'You might not have noticed but it is very late. Even policemen have to sleep. What is it about?'

'What I have to say is for the captain's ears.'

The man weighed up his night visitor. 'Wait here. I will inform the duty officer.'

Grimm wished only to see Salinas but before he could say anything the officer had left his desk and was disappearing round a corner into the depths of the building. Grimm heard boots echoing down a corridor, then voices. The desk officer reappeared. 'This way, *señor*.'

Grimm followed him into an office. He recognised the lieutenant, black leather gloves and all: Damio, the hardcase who had worked him over.

'Accept my apologies for our little recent misunderstanding, *señor*.'

The man was smiling but Grimm said nothing. 'Well,' the man continued, 'what is this all about?'

'I'm told the captain is off duty. Can you tell me his home address? It's kinda important.'

'What is it?'

'The captain told me to keep him informed on certain matters. That's why I am here. And that's why I would like to see him personal.'

'If it's a police matter, you tell me.'

'*Por favore*, Captain Salinas.'

The man looked him over. 'I'm not in the mood for games, *señor*. Wiping away sweat with nothing to do but swat bugs in the heat of a night shift does not leave me in good temper. You tell me, that is the way we do it. I am the senior officer in the *capitan*'s absence.'

Grimm stepped back towards the door. 'I'll leave it until tomorrow.'

'If it is important as you say, *señor*, then you have a problem. The *capitan* has duties elsewhere tomorrow.'

Grimm stopped in the doorway. 'Won't he be in at all?'

'He will not be on the premises until the afternoon maybe. If you will be good enough to tell me the subject of your information, we'll take it from there.'

Grimm thought it over. Stymied. What else could he do? 'There is to be a trial tomorrow,' he began.

'Yes.'

'Well, there's gonna be trouble concerning a witness.'

The man stiffened. 'What do you know about a witness?'

'Enough.'

'Is that all you're saying?'

'Until I see the captain, yes.'

The man pondered then rose. 'You are an obstinate man, *señor*. So be it. Come with me.' He took Grimm to an anteroom. 'You stay here, *señor*,' he said as he fired an oil-lamp on the wall. 'I will see if I can get a message to the chief.'

'*Gracias*.'

Grimm dropped on to the sole chair and looked the place over as the man left. It was bleak and cramped with one window so high up it was impossible to see through. He was beginning to wonder if he'd done the right thing when he heard a key clunk in the lock. He moved swiftly to the door and banged it. 'I'm here to help. There's no call to lock me in.'

Beyond the door the sound of footsteps diminished and he began to prowl round the bare room in frustration. Huh, the way these Mexes did business.

As the minutes built up he resigned himself to an irritating wait. It must have been half an hour later when he heard footsteps again. There was the key in the lock and the door swung open to reveal Damio. 'My apologies for the wait, *señor*. I have been as quick as I could.' His demeanour was more pleasant than when he had left. Grimm put two and two together and figured the man had been put in his place by the chief.

He rose. 'I didn't take kindly to you locking the

door, mister. What was the purpose of that? I come here in good faith to help you guys out.'

'I'm sure you have, *señor*. Sorry about locking the door but it's just routine. You'll be surprised how many *hombres* come to the police with information on serious matters then have second thoughts. I hope it did not disturb you too much. Anyway, come. The chief will see you.'

'Where is he?'

'We are all occupied with the matter of this trial tomorrow. He is on duty elsewhere.'

'Guarding this witness in some hidey-hole?'

'All will be revealed, *señor*. Come.'

Grimm followed him out of the building. They walked down the street and turned down an alley. Soon they were in unsavoury quarters. It was dark with cloud obscuring the moon so Grimm could see very little. They turned another corner and he saw even less when something cracked down on the back of his head and he pitched forward.

Vaguely aware of being tied up, he grunted resistance when some evil-tasting cloth was used to gag him. He was carried some distance, then into a building. Eventually he was dumped against a wall.

'This is perfect.' The voice was familiar. As fuller consciousness returned he recognized it as belonging to the man he had heard at the cotton warehouse: Johnson. 'Letting me know about this was good thinking, Damio.'

The place was dimly lit and the figure was against what light there was, so Grimm still couldn't put a face on the man who was talking. 'Somehow the *hombre* has found out about our plans for tomorrow. Did he tell the desk officer anything?'

'No,' Damio answered. 'I asked him. All he said was that he wanted to see the captain.'

Grimm cursed himself for his own stupidity. He had no one to blame but himself for his predicament. Salinas himself had told him many of the *rurales* were bent.

'The first time he mentioned knowing something about the hit,' Damio went on, 'was when he was talking to me in my office.'

'Good. If the captain finds out about his visit and asks awkward questions you can make up some story.'

'No problem.'

The men lit smokes, then Johnson continued with a satisfied tone lying thick on his voice. 'You know, *amigo*, this kills two birds with one stone. This is the way we'll play it. I know the bozo carries a rifle because I've seen a rifle boot on his rig. Get the gun from his lodgings. As a police officer you won't be questioned about what you're doing there. Pass the gun to me. Tomorrow we'll smuggle him into the Mission. With the padre out of the way there won't be any trouble. I'll use Grimm's rifle for the job and when I've made the hit, you shoot him as I make my getaway. If you have to shoot him twice, then do so. Just as long as he's dead when the chief arrives. You untie him, then you tell your boss you shot the *hombre* as he was coming down from the campanile with the smoking rifle in his hand. When the chief sees him his gun will be by his side, still warm. It'll all tie up neat. It'll take the heat off any search for me and get the nosy gringo out of the way at the same time. Couldn't have worked out better.'

'It would be even better if we killed him beforehand, *señor*.'

Johnson went to a window and moved sacking to look out into the street. 'Yeah, as long as he's alive he's still a wild card in the deck; but I can't risk a shot attracting attention, even out here. There are night patrols. Some straight *rurales* could come investigating and foul things up.'

He moved away from the window. 'Besides the wound would be caked over by the time the chief saw the body. No, you'll have to do it at the proper time.'

Grimm saw him take out a roll and peel off a sizeable wad of bills. 'That's for your trouble, *amigo*. Now fetch me his rifle and then get back to the Bureau like nothing has happened.'

SIXTEEN

The next morning Father Alonso was in the vestry of the Guadelupe Mission counselling a young couple who wished to be married. There was a knock at the door.

'Come in.'

A *peon* whose face he didn't recognize appeared. 'Excuse me, padre. I have an urgent message.'

'What is it, my son?'

'Forgive me. It is Vicente Campo. He is dying, padre. The doctor is with him. Señor Campo wishes you to be at his side to administer the last rites.'

'Vicente Campo? I don't think I know him.'

'He takes mass here at the Mission.'

The priest shook his head. 'My memory is fading with age. I feel deficient in not knowing all my flock. Certainly, my son. I will come directly. Where is he?'

'In his *casa*. Just out of town. I will show you, padre. But hurry.'

'Of course.' The priest turned to his visitors. 'I'm sorry about this, my children. Please excuse me. We shall continue our discussion this afternoon if that is all right with you.'

* * *

Meanwhile Lieutenant Damio had presented himself at Johnson's lodgings. The bandit had prepared everything and was waiting. There was a large rug unrolled beside the still form of Grimm who had been rendered unconscious again and a bag pulled over his head.

'How are you explaining your absence on such an important day?' Johnson asked, as he raised a chest lid.

'Sent in a message that I have a feverish chill.'

Johnson took a couple of monk's robes from the chest. 'Take off your cap and gloves and get this on,' he said, throwing one of the habits at the puzzled police officer. 'You and I are taking holy orders for a spell.'

When they had donned the clothing he pulled the rug nearer Grimm. 'Now help me roll the *hombre* up in this thing.'

* * *

It was a busy day in Juarez. It was known that a big trial was scheduled for the law court that morning. Outside the building there had been a queue for the public seats since early on. Those that couldn't get in were crowded outside hoping for a glimpse of the prisoners. News had leaked out that there was a witness and that he was being brought in under police protection so crowds were lining the street as far back as the plaza.

Such a day meant good business for a pickpocket like little Ricardo. Better than market day. Within an hour he had a couple of pockets rattling with pesos. He usually targeted the well dressed. They were careless and could afford it. He could pull up a pocket flap and put in his little hand without the victim feeling it. Another way was to collide hard with the target as he was turning. The man wouldn't associate the impact with a boisterous street urchin with the removal of his wallet. At least, not until it was too late.

Ricardo had just pulled such a stunt with an elderly *hidalgo* who had had got tired while waiting in the early morning heat and had taken respite on an adobe step. The old man had taken off his sombrero to fan his brow when Ricardo had chosen to run by and fall against him. So accidental did it appear when the little one collided with him that the *hidalgo* apologized as though it were his fault.

'That is all right, *señor*,' the lad had said, hiding a smile, and had scurried with his prize into the crowds. There were two things to do immediately after a dip. Get as far from the victim as possible, and discard incriminating wallets.

Accordingly he weaved his way through the crowds and broke free in an alley. He skipped along the garbage-strewn passageway, looked around to ensure he was not being seen and stopped to check his haul. He was in luck. The wallet was full of bills. He took them out and threw the wallet behind a pile of trash.

Clutching his treasure trove under his poncho he stepped into a doorway to count it. *Caramba,* he was rich! He stuffed them in his back pocket and was about to leave the safety of the doorway when he saw two men carrying a large rug at the end of the alley. They were dressed in the plain habits of monks and he noticed nothing untoward save that the carpet was sagging heavily between them. He gave them no further mind; just waited for them to pass so that he could return to his lucrative business in the main street.

Suddenly the heavy burden escaped the grasp of the monk at the rear. He shouted that he was in trouble and managed to keep a grip of one end of the rug. But some heavy weight inside unravelled the thing and it partially fell to the ground. Enough for Ricardo to see the rug contained a man, an unconscious man.

The other monk cursed in a very unreligious way and the two quickly proceeded to encase the figure once more. Having done so they resumed their journey and disappeared at the far end of the alley.

The incident itself was of interest to the young boy. But even more so because he thought he recognized the unconscious man. He had only caught a brief glimpse as the bearers had been anxious to cover the disclosure of their odd burden but it looked very much like the gringo who earlier had been so generous to him. Yet another oddity: the second monk had snagged his habit as he struggled to get their burden covered and, for a few seconds, had displayed what seemed to be the pants leg of a uniform. What was going on?

SEVENTEEN

The two men turned into the alley alongside the Mission. A *peon* was leaning against the whitewashed wall. He sprang to life on seeing them and ran forward. 'The padre has gone, *señor*. Thinks he is to deliver the last rites to a peasant out of town.'

'Good,' Johnson grunted. He nodded towards a side door to the Mission. 'Now open up that door.' Inside, they unrolled the unconscious Grimm on to the slabbed floor.

The two men took off their cassocks and dropped them on the opened rug. Johnson rolled them up and spoke to the *peon*. 'Now vamoose and get rid of that stuff.'

He adjusted the rifle hanging from his back then bent down to grip Grimm's shoulders. With the *peon* gone and the door closed behind him, the two men hauled the figure up to the landing just below the campanile and dumped it against a wall.

Johnson took the gun from his back and jacked in a cartridge. He threw a look at Damio which said 'This is it', then he loped up the remaining steps. At the top he crouched low and looked over the edge. The campanile gave a commanding view of the plaza and main street. Way below the crowd waited, their expectant buzz wafting upwards. He turned his head: he had clear sight of the entrance to the court house. He checked the position of the sun. To his right above the campanile, it wouldn't interfere with his aim. He ducked back down to minimize the risk of being seen, then, every few seconds, peered back over.

How long would he have to wait? One thing he knew: he felt comfortable with a gun in his hand again. Even if it was someone else's gun. All those weeks of idle masquerade were beginning to eat into his soul. But now, with a gun in his fist and a bullet in the breech he was himself again.

At the bottom of the stairs Damio waited, looking upwards. Near his polished boot tips the trussed up Grimm snuffled slightly as consciousness attempted to get a grip of his brain.

Back at the summit of the campanile Johnson suddenly became aware of a rise in the buzz coming from the crowd and he knew his waiting was over. Once more he raised his head, very slowly. Yes, a group of riders were making their way towards the plaza: a circle of uniforms around a civilian. Huh, in a white shirt the man couldn't have presented a better target. It did not concern him who the fellow was, nor what were the rights and wrongs. He had been paid good dinero to do a job and he would do it.

The professional assassin brought the rifle

into view and lined it up over the parapet. This
was his business and he didn't need to take long.
He simply aimed with a rock-like steadiness and
fired. He slipped the smoking weapon out of
sight as quickly as it had appeared and dipped
down, keeping his eyes on the scene just long
enough to see the target caroom out of the
saddle. A head shot, that was enough.

Just as he had predicted, the faces of
onlookers angled in all directions, confused by
the echoes against the adobe walls. Then, as he
dropped from view, the firecracker diversion
began. He skipped down the stairs and laid the
rifle near Grimm.

'The main business is concluded,' he grunted
to the waiting *federale*. 'All that remains is to tie
up the loose ends.' He nodded at the figure on
the floor. 'OK, *amigo*, you know what to do.'

He swung his legs over the window sill and
began his escape across the roof.

Damio looked down at Grimm and unfastened
his holster flap. He pulled his gun, cocked it and
levelled it at the man's head.

'No, *señor*. You cannot do that!'

It was a high-pitched voice from his side. He
swung round in its direction to see a young boy
peeping from the top of the stairs. What the hell
was a kid doing here?

'*Vamoose, muchacho!*'

Ricardo lowered his head but remained
steadfast. He had been intrigued and the
curiosity of an urchin who lived by street
knowledge had overcome discretion. He did not

know what was going on but he knew it involved his gringo *amigo*. 'You cannot kill a man like that!'

Damio ran to the steps but by the time he had reached the top the lad had descended and disappeared round a corner. The officer began to panic. He couldn't afford the time to chase the urchin all round the Mission. He looked back at Grimm who was just coming to. What was he to do now he had been seen? The hell with it, he would still follow Señor Johnson's plan and shoot the gringo. The kid should know it was more than his life's worth to finger a *federale*. Even if he did blab, it was only a kid's word against his.

He strode towards his victim to ensure it would be a killing shot, but the clatter of heavy boots on stone came from below; then the kid shouting, 'Upstairs. There's a man with a gun!'; followed by the sound of the heavy boots on the stairs. Had to be his fellow police officers.

Caramba, if he killed the man now he wouldn't have time to untie his bonds and that would need explaining. Before he knew it, decision-making was out of his hands when uniformed men with guns in their hands appeared at the top of the stairs.

'What is it, Lieutenant?' one asked.

'Yes, what goes, Damio?' The question was echoed by Captain Salinas who emerged wheezing at the top of the stairs.

'This is the culprit, Capitan,' Damio said, now sweating profusely as he backed towards the window. 'I caught him and tied him up.'

Salinas rolled his bulky form until he was standing above the reviving Grimm. 'And knocked him out too. An extraordinarily fast piece of work, Lieutenant. Especially by some-body supposedly off duty with a fever.'

He looked back at Damio and recognized fear in his eyes.

'That is not true, Capitan.' It was Ricardo who was peering between uniformed legs at the scene. 'There were two of them. They carried the gringo in wrapped in a rug.'

Salinas turned to look at the little boy. 'And who are you, *muchacho*?'

'Ricardo, *señor*.'

'And what have you seen?'

'The two men carried the gringo up here. Somebody fired a shot up there.' He waved vaguely upwards. 'Which is a strange sound to come from a church.' He pointed at Damio. 'I came up the stairs and I saw that man aiming his pistol at the gringo. He was going to kill him, *señor*, but I shouted.'

Salinas turned towards his subordinate but Damio swung his legs over the window sill and clattered on to the roof. The captain moved to the window accompanied by one of his men carrying a gun. The chief's initial reluctance to give the order to fire at his lieutenant enabled the man to get to the end and disappear from view.

'After Damio!' Salinas yelled.

A couple of men made to clamber through the window.

'No, down below, idiots!' the chief chided. 'And don't let him get away.'

As uniformed men headed for the stairs he looked back at Grimm. 'And somebody get that gag off him.'

'What the hell's going on?' Grimm grunted, his eyes struggling to get into focus as his mouth was freed.

'I'm hoping you can tell me, *señor*,' Salinas said.

'There's going to be a shooting,' Grimm said. 'Johnson and your man. They're going to shoot your witness and hang the rap on me.'

'You're too late, *amigo*. It has happened. Sanchez is dead.'

'Jesus. I must have been out longer than I thought.'

'Untie the man's bonds,' Salinas said. 'But keep him covered.'

Grimm staggered to his feet after he had been freed and leant against a wall, cradling his head. He didn't know how much more punishment his skull could take.

'Just exactly who is this Johnson?' the captain asked.

Grimm was having trouble getting his brain working. 'Still don't know what he looks like. But I got a feeling I recognize the voice. Somebody I've seen in town.'

'I know who the other man is, *señor*,' Ricardo said. 'But his name is not Johnson. It is Julio. He is a swamper at the Paradiso Cantina.'

'Yeah,' Grimm said, realization hitting him almost as hard as the previous blow to his head.

'*That's* where I've heard the voice. He's covered his face with whiskers to hide the scarring, but he can't disguise the trouble he has talking.'

'Come with me, *señor*,' Salinas said and headed for the stairs, waving a limp arm at Ricardo. 'And you, *muchacho*.'

EIGHTEEN

Grimm crashed through the doors of the Paradiso and strode across the bar floor. A startled customer looked at him wide-eyed while the proprietor shouted a challenge from the bar. Grimm ignored them both and leapt up the stairs. There were three doors. He kicked open one. Nothing. He kicked open a second. A couple were involved in some activity that engrossed them so much they didn't look up.

He burst through the door of number three. A figure came from the dark recesses into the light of a kerosene lamp hanging from the ceiling. Third time lucky. It was the cantina broom-hack – Julio – Winchy Francisco Johnson – whatever he called himself.

'Hey, what gives?' he challenged. The speech impediment which had originally led Grimm to dismiss the fellow as the local village idiot was now recognizable for what it was: the result of jaw injury.

'You're Johnson,' Grimm challenged. 'It all fits. The voice. The beard covering the smashed-up jaw. Perfect cover.'

'You better get the hell out of here, gringo, or somebody'll be carrying you out.'

Meanwhile an out-of-breath Salinas arrived at the front of the building with two of his men. Stationing them there, he paused to wipe his brow then made his own entry while Ricardo, with no love of policemen, kept his distance.

Upstairs, Grimm was forcing Johnson into a showdown. 'Yeah,' he went on, looking around. 'I recognize the smell of the place. This is where you kept me overnight.'

The man advanced towards him. 'I ain't warning you no more, gringo. You're on private property. You're trespassing.'

'And it was you that battered me about the head a few times. And tried to pin Sanchez's shooting on me.'

Anger spilling over, the bounty hunter leapt forwards swinging a fist which caught the man. The blow knocked Johnson back but he recovered enough to hurl himself at his attacker. Locked in an embrace which was anything but loving they crashed to the floor.

'That'll be enough,' the captain bellowed as he finally entered. He bent forward and hauled Grimm away. Now apart, and in the face of the law, the two men restrained themselves.

The captain stepped in between them and looked at the swamper. 'How long you been here?'

'What's going on?' It was the proprietor who'd followed the policeman up the stairs and was now standing in the doorway.

Without looking behind him the captain threw him a very hard finger. 'Police business. Out.'

The proprietor backed away.

Maintaining his stare at Johnson the police chief repeated his question. 'How long you been here?'

The man waved a hand at a straw pallet in the recesses. 'Just got out of the sack. Had a lot to drink last night. Kinda goes with the job. You know, working in a cantina. First thing I know this crazy man busts in.'

The captain looked the place over. 'This is where you live?'

'If you can call it living.'

'What's your name?'

'Julio.'

'That's what you're calling yourself at the moment,' Grimm interjected. 'But it's an alias while you do your work for the Don. Real name's Johnson.'

'Is it hell? Where you get these loco ideas?'

'You talk like a gringo,' the captain observed.

'No. I am Mexican, *señor*, born and bred. Home town's Guadalajara.'

'You were born in Juarez,' Grimm countered. 'And you got a woman here. Consuela Galinas de Zedari, Don Ruiz's sister.'

'The Señorita Consuela de Zedari? Huh, to be in the company of such a woman is nothing but a dream for a man of my humble circumstances.'

'You still talk like a gringo,' the captain persisted.

The man nodded. 'I spent some time north of

the Rio Grande. My old man, he was Americano.'
He looked across at Grimm who was wandering
around the space. 'Anyways, that's the gringo
who shot the guy on the way to court. What's he
doing here?'

'Oh, yes?' the captain said. 'And how do you
know anybody got killed if you just got up?'

The man rubbed his face. 'It was the shooting
that woke me. I been awake long enough to find
out what happened. They're buzzing with the
story outside. Said something about a gringo had
shot some poor *hombre* in police custody. I was
just going to get my head down again when this
hombre breaks in and leaps on me.'

The captain nodded, then said, 'The gringo
says that you did the killing.'

The man chuckled. 'Figure if I was in his boots
facing a firing squad I'd say something like that
too.'

'I seen you around,' the captain went on.
'What else you do besides swamping?'

'Most anything that comes up.'

Grimm butted in with 'Including shooting a
guy for a big handout.'

The man looked back at the lawman. 'Listen, I
don't have to take this, Captain. Just coz I'm a bit
of a bum, ain't no reason to let an *hombre* like him
come mooching round my place and making
accusations. Ain't right.'

'The captain's investigating a murder,' the
bounty hunter said. 'Seems to me it's up to him to
say what's right and wrong about procedures.'
As he spoke, Grimm was rummaging under

blankets. His delving revealed a gunbelt. He
picked it up and unravelled it, showing two
holstered guns. 'Look at this, Captain. A brace of
guns. Smart shooting irons at that. Remember
what you said of me, Captain? A man's guns say a
lot about him. There's a well-oiled rifle here too.'
He pointed to the latter which he unearthed from
the blanket. 'Is this the kind of weaponry toted by
a saloon swamper?'

Johnson grabbed the belt from him. 'Get your
filthy gringo hands off those things. They are
keepsakes. Guns belonged to my old man. He
rode nighthawk on herds Stateside. That's the
way he made his living. He was a good man.' He
moved forward to prevent Grimm making
further investigations but was too late.

The bounty hunter pulled out a further bulky
object. 'And where does a saloon swamper earn
this kind of dough?' He held up a massive roll of
bills for the captain's perusal. 'Like I said. Living
like a pig and swamping cantinas is a cover while
he's in town as a paid hit-man.'

'Hey,' Johnson snapped, putting out his hand.
'That's my nest egg.'

The captain motioned for Grimm to pass it to
him and the bounty hunter obliged.

Salinas caught the wad. 'This amount of money
needs explaining.'

'My old man left it me when he passed on.'

'You'll have to do better than that,' the chief
rejoined looking around the room. 'A cow-
prodder leaving dinero on this scale? Fact is, none
of what you've said so far holds much water.'

Johnson ignored the implied query and cradled the gunbelt as though in protection of his property. 'You ain't got no right to touch my stuff.'

The chief riffled through the bills while at the other side of the room Grimm continued his search. With both men temporarily occupied Johnson grabbed his chance. In one flowing movement of an experienced gunny he cocked and fired one of the pistols while still in its holster. The first bullet took Salinas as the nearest target and he slumped.

The second was meant for Grimm but the holstered gun, surrounded by its rig made it a clumsy weapon for accuracy across the greater distance. Grimm was on the floor behind the pallet as the second slug holed the wooden wall above his head.

Johnson struggled to get the gun clear of the holster so he could finish off the bounty hunter but there were shouts from the police outside that changed the gunman's priorities. Surprise and indecision registered on his face. But only for a second. He looked up and saw the kerosene lamp hanging from the ceiling. In one movement he whanged it to the floor and scurried through a back door.

The fuel spewing over the matting, the place was ablaze in seconds. Grimm leapt from cover and saw the police chief groaning on the floor, flames licking his boots and his face bronzed in the light of the burning. The place was a tinder box. There was no chance of pursuing Johnson.

He took a grip of the big man and began hauling him towards the door. Flames grabbed insatiably at everything so that by the time he got his burden on to the landing smoke was stinging his nostrils. He thought he heard a muffled bang coming from the rear. Had the police seen Johnson and fired at him? But, given the crackling of the fire, it could have been anything.

The other occupants had made hasty exits and, at the top of the stairs, he was met by officers who helped him get the police chief downstairs. Clear of the building he bent down hands on knees, grabbing for air. When he had finally coughed the choking stuff from his lungs he looked down at Salinas who was on the ground still clutching the wad of bills.

'Give me a gun,' Grimm said.

Salinas hesitated.

'Haven't you seen and heard enough for Christ's sake?' the bounty hunter said, pointing back at the smoking building. 'That's your man.'

The police chief thought on it, nodded then waved a hand at the nearest uniformed man. 'Give him your gun. And give him all the back up he needs.' Then to the rest of his men he said, 'Surround the area. We're looking for a bearded *hombre*.'

Grimm took the weapon, a heavy one-piece military model, and ran down the alley alongside the burning taberna. At the rear he saw a uniformed body. It was Damio, a bullet in the skull. So Grimm had heard a shot after Johnson had broken out. Looked like the double-dealing officer had been panicking and Johnson had dispensed with him in the most obvious way. Grimm had only one regret as he looked at the body: that he himself had not had a chance to repay the bastard for the beating he had given him. Anyway, more relevant to the present, the bloodied corpse showed that Johnson had been this way. Well, the bozo was a quick mover. He'd had no more than a few minutes, but time enough to get rid of a crony who was of no further use, and to make himself scarce.

Wielding the gun, Grimm appraised the backs of the buildings. Hell, the critter could be anywhere. Mind, with the fire in the taberna out of control and certain to spread to adjacent buildings, the varmint would be heading out of town if he had any sense. Grimm looked up and down the alleyway that ran parallel to the street. No sign.

Which way? Fifty-fifty chance. With a lurid red glow behind him he loped down the alley.

He emerged from the alley into a small plaza from which radiated streets and further alleys. He came to a stop and checked off the possible routes. A few *peons* going about their business but otherwise zilch. Head thumping from the beating it had been getting, he stood still, breathing heavy but managing to voice audible expletives, the gun hanging heavy and useless in his hand.

Then, a familiar voice: 'He went that way, *señor*.' It was Ricardo, his arm extended towards one of the alleys.

'Where's it lead?'

'Out of town along the Rio.'

Grimm made to run in the indicated direction but the young lad added some extra information. 'He was on a horse, *señor*.'

So that's how he'd got away so fast.

Grimm clattered to a halt on the plaza slabs. 'Then I need one, don't I! Any ideas, kid?'

Ricardo thumbed a street. 'There's a hitchrail full of them round the corner. *Mucho caballeros* are in town today for the trial.' With that he scuttled off in the indicated direction. 'Leave it to Ricardo, *señor*.'

Seconds later he reappeared leading a tall black stallion in ornate Mexican rig. Grimm secured the gun in his belt and took the reins. '*Gracias, muchacho*.'

Out of town he found himself riding parallel with the Rio Grande as it wound its leisurely way across the bleak landscape. He cast his mind over the possibilities about where Johnson would be heading. One possibility was the Libertad. But that would necessitate swinging south. So as he rode, Grimm threw regular glances in that direction. But, as ahead, he saw no rider.

Just scatterations of rocks and clutches of cacti.

Gaining more confidence with the strange animal, he urged it onward. It was a good specimen. Tall, strong, responsive. The little street urchin knew his horseflesh.

He looked back at Juarez. The fire had really taken a grip; he could see the smoke from this distance. He was straining his eyes once more to the south, when a gun report fire-crackered the stillness.

Lowering his head he reined in hard. He swung down and dashed for the cover of cacti. Not the safest of shields but the only thing available. For a second he closed his eyes, held his forehead in his hand and breathed deeply. He was nettled with himself. If he'd have been his true self he wouldn't have allowed Johnson to get the drop on him like that. It was just dawning on him that his head was still fuzzy from all the bashing it had been getting. Judas Priest, his skull must be as bumpy as a trail-cook's colander. One compensation: Johnson must be feeling the pressure; otherwise he wouldn't have missed a sitting duck like he just had.

Proned against the bole of an old saguaro Grimm pulled out the gun given to him by the policeman and checked the loads. One thing he knew: the only ammo he had was in the chamber, so he couldn't enter into a prolonged showdown. Slowly he peered from cover, watching for the next shot, sure that it would come.

And it did. He withdrew just as a bullet whanged into the plant splintering the surface near his face. But his split second view had been enough to locate Johnson firing from behind a low clump of rock.

He took a deep breath, then ran to where the cacti were thicker. Weaving right and left, he made it to fresh cover. Closer, he could now make out the figure of his adversary more clearly.

He tried another dash, saw flame spurt. But he

felt a searing pain in his left arm and pitched
forward, some distance short of another cactus.
As he hit the ground he kept his eyes on his
assailant, saw the gun raised, primed to send a
last bullet into Grimm's head.

Fortunately, the way the bounty hunter had
fallen, his gun arm was outstretched in line and
he fired instinctively. He didn't know whether he
had been on target, but he saw the figure move
abruptly. Not sure, he fired once more, this time
seeing the man fall.

Grimm waited, then slowly got to his feet.
Johnson was still, his rifle fallen from his grasp.
The bounty hunter approached warily. Then
Johnson made a lunge for his gun, but Grimm
shot at it, his slug slamming into the weapon's
stock swinging it several feet across the sandy soil
away from the desperado's clutching fingers.

Cautiously Grimm continued to step nearer.
Johnson raised his trunk in an ungainly fashion
and tried yet again to reach his weapon. Anxious
to take his man alive, Grimm delayed firing a
further time. But there was no need to pull
trigger again. Johnson's movement was a last,
hopeless show of effort; he struggled and merely
fell on his rifle to lie crumpled and still over the
thing.

Up close Grimm hesitantly turned the man
over. Johnson fell back, unseeing eyes wide
open. Grimm had seen eyes like that many times
before. Unnecessarily he checked the man's
pulse.

He remained hunkered down, contemplating

the figure of the mean sinner that had brought him all the way to Mexico. However he only stayed on his haunches for a few seconds for, with the evaporation of danger, the soreness in his left arm commanded attention. He laid down his pistol and shucked off his jacket to investigate. No problem. One of Johnson's slugs had been close enough to burn the outer flesh; sore as Jehosophat but no blood.

OK, to matters in hand. He looked northward. The Rio Grande was still there, a couple of hundred yards away. From his standpoint, it looked shallow enough to ford without hitch. He could do it now. Nothing stood in his way of heading back. It would mean losing the horses and gear he had left at the lodging-house – he would miss the comfortable feel of his Army .44s – but it would be worth it. Beyond Mexican jurisdiction on the other side of the water there was three grand waiting for him. All he had to do was sling the bozo over his saddle. But he had to move fast.

He looked back in search of Johnson's horse and his heart sank at the sight of uniforms bearing down on him. He saw something else too, this time in his mind: another bounty slipping inexorably from his grasp. The lesson of recent times: there was no straight path to success.

Resigning himself to whatever fate had in store, he retrieved and holstered the gun.

'He's all yours, *compadres*,' he said as the officers drew rein.

NINETEEN

Hat respectfully in hand, Grimm followed the nun down the adobe-walled corridor. She stopped outside a door and ushered him into a room where Salinas's bulk was weighing down a bed.

'He has to remain quiet so don't say anything to upset him,' she whispered to the visitor. 'And don't be too long. The more he rests, the quicker he will be returning home.'

'When will that be, Sister?'

'The doctor says only a matter of days if there are no complications.'

'Thank you, Sister.'

As the door closed he crossed the room and sat on a chair beside the bed. 'How you doing, Captain?'

The police chief shook his hand and grimaced with the movement. 'Bullet went straight through the leg. Damn painful and the medico says I'll probably end up with a bit of a limp, but it could have been a lot worse. But it would have been a helluva lot worse if you hadn't dragged me outa that place, I know that.'

'I just happened to have been there. Hadn't have been me, somebody would have got you out. Your men were outside.'

'Huh, dozy goatherders. I needed getting out fast and you did it, *amigo.*'

Grimm shrugged off the conversation. 'Anyways, how's the case against Ruiz progressing?'

'Good news. The proprietor of the Paradiso gave me a piece of paper that Johnson had given to him with the instruction to pass it to the authorities should anything befall him. The document bears Johnson's signature and declares that if something happened to him he wished to make it known that he had been paid by Don Ruiz to kill Sanchez.'

'How will a document like that stand up in court?'

'By Our Lady, you never can tell with lawyers. The signature hasn't been witnessed, so its authenticity will be questioned by the defence. But there's the proprietor's statement that it was handed to him by Johnson so I think I should be able to make something stick. If I can't, it won't be through lack of trying. Anyways, even if I can't go the whole hog, it'll be a first nail in the coffin of Don Ruiz's downfall. At least it'll get him into court and start the ball rolling in the right direction.'

'Bad luck that I planted Johnson. I didn't intend it that way. My head was all fuzzed up and he was throwing lead at me. Would have helped you clinch things if I could have taken him alive.'

'Not necessarily. Johnson would have found

himself being represented by top-notch lawyers financed by Ruiz. Knowing which side his bread was buttered he would have denied working for the Don. And in those circumstances the Paradiso man would not have felt obliged to pass on Johnson's incriminating statement. So things aren't too bad the way they fell.'

'Well, I'm glad things are turning your way.'

Salinas eyed him. 'You didn't just come to enquire about my health and business, did you?'

'I'd be a liar if I said yes. Fact is, I would be obliged to know something on the matter of claiming bounty on Johnson. The way it fell it was me that put the final stopper on him. As you know, it was to get his hide that I came to Mexico in the first place. And it's time I was heading back across the old Rio Grande.'

'It is true you killed him, *amigo*, but you must know you can't have the body.'

'Captain, the only way I get paid is for physically delivering him Stateside. Dead or alive. Hell, now he's dead he's no use to you.'

Salinas shrugged. 'My apologies, *Señor* Grimm, but it's out of my hands. Whatever Johnson did outside of Mexican jurisdiction following his faked death is not my prime concern. His shooting of Sanchez, not to mention his previous crimes for which he has not been brought to book, were committed in Mexico. So, the body belongs here.' He pondered on it, then added, 'Of course, I could sign an affidavit to the effect that you were instrumental in his apprehension. If that would help?'

Grimm shook his head. 'Don't think it would pan out. I have to physically present the corpse to the US legal authority. That's the only way it works.'

'Yes, I realize. It would not be the way out for you. The American authorities would need to know the dead man was positively their man and I have no way of verifying that he was the man that you sought for crimes in the US.'

Grimm remained silent, then Salinas pointed to a cupboard. 'There's a box of cigars in there. Get it out for me, would you?'

His mind on other things the visitor obliged mechanically, passing it to the patient who broke the seal and raised the wooden lid. 'You'll join me, *señor*?'

The offer acted like a magnet, deflecting the elements of Grimm's thought, reminding him of a pleasure of which he'd been deprived. They were large, quality cigars and looking at them caused him to realize he couldn't remember the last time he'd had a smoke. 'Sure thing,' he said. 'I'm fresh out of my makings.'

'Yes. I heard about that.'

Salinas did the honours with a match and they were both soon wreathed in smoke.

'Cuban?' Grimm murmured with satisfaction as he savoured the thing.

'The best, *señor*.'

The bounty hunter went to the window and looked out contemplatively as he drew on the cigar. 'Out of interest,' he said after an interval, 'where will they be burying Johnson?'.

Salinas's jaw dropped. '*Señor*, now I think that I

can safely say that you and I are friends – but you would find out what it is like to have a mountain fall upon you if you started digging up bodies.' Then he chuckled. 'You never give up, do you?'

Grimm echoed the chuckle but with less evidence of humour in the tone, then nodded at the view through the window as though he could see all the way back to the States. 'A hell of a way to come, to have to go back empty-handed.'

There was silence then the captain said, 'It may not have to be so.'

Grimm turned. 'No?'

'I am thinking aloud and talking between four walls, you understand,' the captain said in a lowered voice.

'Yeah?'

'Even if I can pin something on Don Ruiz as I hope to do, those three murderers still go free. Sanchez was the only witness to their crime so legally the matter ends there. Their case is closed – officially. Now that is a pity because we are pretty sure that the three have perpetrated many other killings and atrocities. But this last murder was the first time we'd really got something positive on them. They are scum.' His voice took on a reflective tone, the words coming out more slowly. 'So, if they were to be eliminated, quietly and off the record, the Bureau would be grateful.'

'How grateful?'

'In Mexican currency the equivalent of, say, a grand apiece.'

'I thought the law authorities down here were short of funds?'

The captain winked. 'You have not been here long enough to know of, what in your language, is called "the bite". When apprehended, even for the smallest misdemeanour, our good citizens are prepared to pay, shall we say, unofficial fines, to be let off the hook. It is expected. What one might call a tradition. Now, the arresting officer takes the main proportion of the bite of course, but a percentage often goes into a fund for contingencies. There will be enough to finance a contract on three vermin as I have suggested. That is all such a man would need to know.'

'This man that you are talking about, why would you be making such an offer to him? You don't have to.'

'A way of saying *gracias*.' The police chief looked up at the ceiling and watched his smoke rise on the still air. 'Moreover I appreciate the position of a gringo bounty hunter, thwarted in a foreign country. He enforces law in his own way. At the end of the day he and I are basically on the same side of the fence.' He looked back at the bounty hunter. 'The successful completion of such a contract would mean that this man would not be leaving our country with empty saddle-bags.'

Grimm thought on it. Three grand. Not enough to put the account book ahead given the punishment his skull had been taking, but some compensation for the earlier fouled-up operations. Enough to pay bills; and tide him over while he put his mind to fixing up his next operation. And enough to drop a grand into Dwight Miller's lap. Plus some man-sized fistfuls of silver dollars for the street kid.

'This man that you are talking about,' he said. 'It could be that he once spent the night locked up with with these three bozos. Snag is it was dark and he couldn't see them clearly enough to remember faces.'

The captain puffed reflectively. 'No problem. I will be on my feet in a couple of days. I have to take it easy according to the *medico* but a short visit to my office will not be out of order. Now I have there a file. It lists all the past atrocities for which the three bandidos have evaded capture. Now, if a man capable of handling them was interested, I could give him copies of their pictures and descriptions.'

Grimm was enjoying his cigar, reminding himself of the taste of good tobacco. He nodded at the open box. 'Would there be a box of cigars in it too?'

* * *

That was all a long time ago. Yellowing newspaper clippings from the period note that three bandits charged with murder were released from Juarez Jail for lack of evidence. Those same file clippings also record that shortly afterwards, one by one, they were discovered, each having been mysteriously but cleanly despatched to meet his Maker. The bodies were duly identified by the authorities – but to this day it has never been learned who dispensed the justice that the renegades had evaded in court.